# Orders to Vietnam

# Orders to Vietnam

❀ ❀

A NOVEL OF HELICOPTER WARFARE

by

W. E. Butterworth

LITTLE, BROWN AND COMPANY

BOSTON                    TORONTO

LIBRARY OF CONGRESS CATALOG CARD NO. 68–15387

FOURTH PRINTING

*Published simultaneously in Canada*
*by Little, Brown & Company (Canada) Limited*

PRINTED IN THE UNITED STATES OF AMERICA

This book is for Cliff, who is the closest thing I've ever had to a little brother. Cliff was raised on a farm that's been in his family since the land was owned by the Indians. He's used to working hard with his hands a full day under the hot sun. His idea of a good time is to eat outdoors by a stream, while his children and a herd of Black Angus examine each other through a fence. Cliff is a devoted son, a good husband, a proud father, and a devout member of the Episcopal Church. He has good reason to hate war, and a greater familiarity with it than most people.

For Clifford Merritt Walker, Jr., Signal Corps, United States Army, who as a Captain assigned to the 170th Aviation Company, earned the Distinguished Flying Cross and I don't know how many other medals for courage and devotion to duty while commanding first a section, and then a platoon, of Armed Hueys flying out of Pleiku, Vietnam.

My wife and my kids are grateful, Little Brother — and so am I.

W. E. BUTTERWORTH

*Fairhope, Alabama*
*January, 1968*

# Orders to Vietnam

# ❁ 1 ❁

* * * * * * *
EXTRACT
* * * * * * *

43.    WOJG BYRNES, Wilson C W-675002 reld asg
Hq & Hq Co Stu Regt USAAVNS this sta trfd WP on
recpt 17th Repl Bn Tan Son Nhut AFB Saigon Repub S
Vietnam for furth asgmt w/i USARVN.  AUTH:  TWX
OCPers 45301 Subj: WORWAC Grad List Asgmt.  7 DDALV.
PCS.  TDN.  Approp: S-99-99999.  Tvl by Comm AT
dir.  Off will tvl in Class "A" smr unif.  Civ Cloth
may be taken at off optn.  Mail should be addressed
nm, rk, ser no "trans off, 17th Repl Bn, APO 96267
San Fran Calif" HOR: Apt 1507 The Ilikanai,
Honolulu Hawaii.

* * * * * * *
            BY COMMAND OF GENERAL BURDETTE M. ALLEN
OFFICIAL:
        MERRITT A. CHARLES
        COLONEL, GSC
        CHIEF OF STAFF

IN PLAIN language, these orders meant that he, Bill Byrnes, was on his way to Vietnam. The WOJG stood for Warrant Officer Junior Grade. He wasn't that yet, but it was only a matter of minutes now. Bill shifted on his folding wooden chair in the Alabama heat. Then, as his group was called, he stood up, stuffed the orders into his pocket and marched in file with the others up the aisle of the small auditorium to the stage.

He stood at attention beside the platform as the men before him mounted the steps and walked across the stage to get their commissions. Out of the corner of his eye he could see the first rows of chairs, filled with wives, parents, girl friends — all intent on picking out their own from the khaki-clad ranks of the graduating class.

On this day of graduation from the Army Aviation School, Bill Byrnes was nineteen years old and stood five feet eight and one-half inches tall. As a warrant officer junior grade he would, as outlined officially in Army Regulations and unofficially and somewhat more clearly in the *Officers' Guide,* rank immediately above the sergeants major of the Army (the highest-ranking enlisted men) and below chief warrant officers and commissioned officers. He would be entitled to a salute from all enlisted men, would be afforded the privileges of the officers' open mess and the bachelor officers' quarters. Officers and enlisted men alike would call him "Mr. Byrnes."

Bill would be glad to drop the title of Warrant Officer Candidate, known to one and all as WOC. The tired old joke would no longer apply. "WOC? What's a WOC? Why a WOC is something you frow at a wabbit."

In a very real sense, Bill Byrnes had done well in the Army. He had had less than a year of college, and he had

4

been in the Army now just over ten months. In that time he had graduated with the first platoon of "Alpha" Company, Third Training Regiment, Armored Replacement Training Center, Fort Knox, Kentucky, and from the U. S. Army Primary Helicopter School, Camp Wolters, Texas. And today he was graduating from the U. S. Army Aviation School at Fort Rucker, Alabama.

The line in front of Bill dwindled. Soon it was his turn, and he climbed the steps and headed for General Allen. The general was a tall, crew-cut, young-looking brigadier. On his chest were five full rows of ribbons, as well as the parachutist's and expert combat infantryman's insignias and a set of aviator's wings.

General Allen had treated each of the other brand-new warrant officers and aviators in WORWAC 7–97 alike. He had shaken each man's hand as he handed him his commission and had said exactly the same words to each: "Congratulations and good luck."

To Warrant Officer Byrnes, however, he said: "Well, Billy, it's good to finally see you."

"Thank you, sir," Bill said, almost slipping and saying, "Uncle Bert." General Allen wasn't really his uncle, but he was as close to it as possible without ties of blood or marriage.

"I'll see you after the ceremony," General Allen said.

"Yes, sir," Bill said, after a moment's hesitation. There was no reason why he shouldn't. He wasn't warring with Burdette Allen, even if General Allen was his father's best friend. Furthermore, now that he was through school and had his orders to Vietnam, there could be no question that seeing General Allen was anything but a visit to someone who had known him all his life.

The general turned to meet the next man and Bill made his way off the stage. As he did so, a woman in the first row of guest chairs stood up and walked over to him, her wide-brimmed hat flopping. There was no chance of avoiding her. She kissed him on the cheek. This was Mrs. Allen. Aunt Marge.

"I'm sorry your dad's not here," she said.

"I'm not," Bill said.

"Is it really that bad between you and your father?" she asked.

"I'm a disgrace to my heritage," Bill said. He said it louder than he had intended, and people looked at them. "Didn't Mother tell you?"

"Shhhh," she said. "Not here."

That's right, Bill thought. Not here. Maintain the facade. An officer's dignity. She pulled him over to a chair. Not where he had been sitting before the ceremony began, but one of the chairs with nice neat white cotton coverings, reserved for senior officers and their families. It wasn't the first time he'd sat in such chairs. As a toddler, he'd sat on Grandma's lap on chairs reserved for Lieutenant General Wilson C. Byrnes and family. Two years ago, he'd sat on chairs reserved for Major General W. C. Byrnes, Jr., and family.

In one sense, Bill Byrnes had been in the Army about ten months. In another sense, he had been in the Army all of his nineteen years. He was an Army brat, the son of an Army brat, the grandson of an Army brat. The trouble was that he had marched away from the Long Gray Line after two months at West Point. He had quit. And he, the direct lineal descendant of seven generations of Army officers, had actually had to be drafted into the service! He was now a warrant officer only because he had decided this was the best way to put in his two-year hitch. He wasn't especially proud of himself for having successfully completed the aviation course.

Flying, he had decided, was about as difficult as learning how to scuba dive. And learning how to soldier, how to conduct himself as an officer? It was second nature to a boy who'd grown up on Army posts around the world, who had spent four years at a military prep school. The school inspections when he was fourteen had been tougher, more chicken, than they were at Fort Rucker. If he had wanted, he could have worn medals for expert rifleman and expert pistol shot. His skill with weapons had awed some of the other WOCs, many of whom, he knew, had never fired a gun until they came into the service. He had first fired the Service pistol at age eight. When he was twelve, the sergeant in charge of the post pistol team at Fort Hood had spent days with him teaching him how to shoot. He'd been an expert with the rifle and the pistol before the first faint whisker had appeared on his cheeks.

For something to do, he reached into the breast pocket of his tunic and took out his orders again. The abbreviations and symbols might baffle others, but Bill read it as if it had been spelled out in longhand: Warrant Officer Junior Grade Wilson C. Byrnes was relieved from assignment to Headquarters and Headquarters Company, Student Regiment, United States Army Aviation School, at this station, transferred and will proceed on receipt of these orders to the 17th Replacement Battalion, Tan Son Nhut Air Force Base, Saigon, Republic of South Vietnam, for further as-

7

signment with the U. S. Army in Vietnam. Authority for the order was a teletype message from the Office of the Chief of Personnel number 45301, and the subject: Warrant Officer Rotary Wing Aviation Course Graduation List Assignment. Seven days delay en route (leave) was authorized. PCS. TDN meant that it was a permanent change of station, and that the travel was deemed necessary in the interests of the United States. The appropriation, the source of the funds, was S99–99999, the general operating fund for the Army's expenses. Travel by commercial air transportation was directed. He was to travel in a dress, or Class "A," summer uniform. If he wanted to, he could take civilian clothing with him. Mail should be sent to him at the Army Post Office in San Francisco, stating that he was a transient officer in the 17th Replacement Battalion. HOR meant Home of Record. The Ilikanai was an apartment building in Honolulu.

And in that apartment building his mother was living, while her husband — his father — was off in Vietnam. He could picture the apartment door, light green with a small neat white engraved card centered on its shiny surface: Wilson Campbell Byrnes, Jr., Major General, United States Army.

Bill had no intention of traveling in his uniform, at least not until he was on the last, Hawaii-Hickham Field-Tan Son Nhut leg of his journey. Just as soon as this graduation ceremony was over, he was going to ship all of his uniforms but one to Vietnam. He would buy his own ticket and travel to Hawaii as Mr. (Civilian Type) Byrnes, and then turn his Army-issue ticket in for a refund.

He knew the ropes. He might be a new warrant officer,

but he knew almost as much about the Army as the old-time warrants had known. Until Army Aviation got to be a big thing in the service, the warrant officer grades hadn't been handed out to youngsters not old enough to vote. In the old Army, you got to be a warrant officer after you had maybe fifteen, sixteen years of good, even outstanding, enlisted service. Then you were made a warrant officer both as sort of a reward for past services rendered and as recognition that you were an expert in some sort of military skill.

Personally, Bill Byrnes couldn't see that much difference between driving a helicopter and driving a tank. Tank commanders were sergeants, although their tanks cost just about as much as a helicopter, and they had just about the same degree of responsibility. But the Army, working in its own mysterious way, had decided that helicopter pilots should be warrant officers. Bill knew that it was impossible to fathom the Army's reasons sometimes, and that the way to success was to just let yourself be carried along with the tide, like a paper cup floating in the ocean.

They had told him at basic training that he was qualified to go either to Officer Candidate School or to Flight School. Flight School would be easier, Bill had decided, and on top of that, pilots drew flight pay. If he could save some of that it would be easier when he took off his uniform and went back to school. After he'd quit West Point and entered college, he'd had to resign because he couldn't support himself.

That, of course, had been reason enough for the draft board to get him. He had lost his student's exemption when he had dropped out of school. There was a distinction in Bill's mind between serving as a professional soldier (he wanted none of that) and serving as a draftee. It was only fair that a citizen be called upon to serve a couple of years in uniform. But just because his father and his grandfather and his great-grandfather had gone to West Point, he couldn't see where that gave the country the right to his services for the rest of his life.

There had been words between Bill and his father about West Point. Strong words. His father was not used to being argued with, and he was not at all used to defiance from his family. The general's idea of reasoning together was to expose, one at a time, what he called logical points. He was wholly unable, it had turned out, to understand that something which was logical to him made no sense whatever to his son. He had told Bill that the choice was his, but that if he gave up West Point without giving West Point a chance, he wanted nothing more to do with him.

"If that's the way you want it." Bill had said. "I don't *want* to be an officer. I want to be a marine biologist."

"In that case, I promise you I'll do everything in my power to have you transferred to Annapolis."

"I don't want to *be* in the service. Can't you understand that?"

"No, I can't," his father had said, icily. The look he gave his son had withered senior colonels. It did not wither his son. Finally, he said, "You understand your alternatives?"

"Yes, sir."

His father walked out of the room. At the door he turned and, red in the face and yet somehow suggesting that he was on the verge of crying, he said, "You're a disgrace to your heritage. I'm ashamed, Bill, I really am ashamed of you."

That was the last time he'd seen or heard from his father. When his mother wrote, she simply said that his father was "well." There had been no money from home, although he knew that if he had asked for some his mother would have sent it to him, no matter how strongly his father felt. For that reason, knowing that he could get it, he had been unable to ask for it.

All things considered, he had done rather well after leaving West Point. He'd been drafted only three weeks after he dropped out of college temporarily to earn some tuition money. So he hadn't lost much time. Now he could put in his two years' service, not counting the ten months it had taken him to get through Flight School, and be saving money at the same time. He would have this money, plus the GI Bill, to finish school with.

Bill was not overly excited about being a duly rated rotary wing aviator, or a new warrant officer, or even about going to Vietnam. The only thing that really bothered him about Vietnam was the possibility that he might run into his father. His father was certain to take Bill's new warrant officer status as evidence that he had regretted the decision he'd made about West Point. He would be sure to look on him as the prodigal son, returning to the fold.

If anything, Bill's ten months in uniform had convinced him that he really wanted no part of the Army, that he really wasn't cut out to be a soldier. Maybe it was terrible, but he really hoped that he could serve his time in Vietnam without encountering his father.

That would be less likely now that General Allen knew where he was, and where he was going.

On the platform, the last graduate received his envelope and handshake from the general, who then began to deliver the graduation address. Bill had heard the same sort of speech delivered by a baker's dozen of different generals, in schools running from Officer Candidate School to Cooks & Bakers. The speaker always took the line that whoever was being graduated represented an indispensable part of the Army team. However valid this argument might be, Bill had heard it before, thought it was redundant, and therefore didn't pay very much attention.

Then there came the familiar voice, yelling "Attention." Bill jumped to his feet, thinking about the Russian Pavlov and his studies and experiments with reflex action. He was just like one of the Russian's dogs. They salivated automatically when a bell rang, and he jumped to attention when someone made that noise. He was one of the first on his feet. It wasn't, he thought, that he was a better soldier than any of the others, just that he had been conditioned to that reflex longer.

Out of the corner of his eye, he saw General Allen leave by the side door of the small auditorium, the door held for him by his aide-de-camp. When the general left, the silence was broken by excited conversation and the sound of laughter.

He looked at Mrs. Allen. What was he supposed to do now? He knew, because he'd been drilled in this all his life, too.

"May I see you to your car?" he asked, politely.

"Thank you."

Her car, of course, was the general's car. He offered her his arm and led her toward the door through which General Allen had disappeared. He held it open for her, and followed her outside.

The general was in the car, and his aide was sitting in the front seat. Bill guided Mrs. Allen toward the rear door, which was held open by a sergeant. The sergeant saluted. Bill returned it. Then the sergeant said, "Congratulations, Billy."

Bill looked at him closely for the first time. "Hiya, Irish," he said, and there was a tight feeling in his throat. Master Sergeant Patrick Finnegan had been with Burdette M. Allen since Korea, when he'd been the sergeant major of the battalion Allen commanded. Sergeant Irish Finnegan had taught Billy Byrnes to drive a car, and a great deal more.

Now Finnegan had his hand out, as if he wanted something.

General Allen spoke, his voice flat but very clear: "Give Irish his dollar, Mr. Byrnes, and get in the car."

"Yes, sir," Bill said. Another old Army tradition. The first time a newly commissioned officer was saluted by an enlisted man, he had to give that soldier a dollar.

Bill took a dollar from his pocket and handed it over.

"Thank you, sir," Sergeant Finnegan said. "And good luck to you, sir." He saluted again and then waited until Bill had gotten into the car, so that he could shut the door after him. Then he trotted around to the driver's seat, and drove slowly away from the auditorium.

The general's car, with its silver star on a red bumper plate, was entitled to a salute. The new warrant officers gathered around the door of the auditorium saluted, and more than one of them recognized Wee Willy Byrnes riding in the back seat with the general.

At least, Bill thought, I won't have to go into long explanations about the whys and wherefores of this. They'll be off the post in an hour. And when we get to Vietnam, this will be ancient history.

"Mr. Byrnes," the general said, "this is my aide-de-camp, Lieutenant Wallace."

"How do you do, sir?" Bill said, politely. The aide turned around in the seat.

"How are you, Mr. Byrnes?" he said. "I'm glad to finally meet you."

Bill wondered what he meant by that, and as if reading his mind, the aide went on. "I've been keeping track of you here," he said.

"Is that so?" Bill said, trying to keep the anger out of his voice.

"Between me and the lieutenant, Billy," Sergeant Finnegan said, "we knew it every time you hiccuped."

"I see," Bill said.

"I was your dad's aide in Saigon," Wallace offered.

"That's a sore subject, Charley," the General said. "Change it."

"Yes, sir," the aide said.

"What do you have to do before clearing the post, Bill?" the general asked.

"Ship my stuff, sir," Bill said.

"You're packed?"

"Yes, sir. And then I've got to pick up my ticket and get to the airport."

"You're on Southern 117 to Atlanta," the aide-de-camp said, "and your reservations are confirmed to Honolulu via United to San Francisco and Northwest Orient to Honolulu."

"Irish'll take you to the airport," the general said. "There'll be enough time."

"Time for what, sir?"

"There are a lot of people on this post, Billy," the general said, "who have really gone out of their way not to see you until now. They're waiting for you at the house."

Not only my father, Bill thought, but everybody has got the wrong idea. I'm *not* the prodigal returning.

There were thirty-odd people at the quarters of General Allen, ranging in grade from Sergeant Finnegan to the post surgeon, now a colonel, who as a captain had been present when Wilson Campbell Byrnes III had been born.

There was a cake, elaborately decorated with sugar statues. There was a sugar statue of a man on a horse, his saddle blanket correctly decorated with three stars. That was Grandfather Byrnes. There was a Patton tank, complete with two-starred identification tag. That was Bill's father. And there was a sugar helicopter, and its pilot, complete with warrant officer's brown and gold bar.

I can't tell these people, Bill thought, but they're all wrong. What I'm going to do is go to Vietnam and then I'm coming back to the States and I'm going to take off my uniform, once and for all.

## ❀ 2 ❀

THERE WAS an aura of unreality about the whole business of being a soldier, a pilot, and on the way to war. It was far more like coming home from military school. His mother met him at the Honolulu airport as she'd met him there a half-dozen times before, and they drove to the apartment with her at the wheel of the family car as they had done before. Bill's father had always been reluctant about his driving the car, and his father's influence was there, and strong, even if General Byrnes were thousands of miles away.

"I'd better drive," his mother had said when they got to the car and he put his hand out for the keys. He didn't argue. It wasn't important.

He arrived on a Sunday and he left on a Sunday. He spent most of the week sitting on the beach, or trying, and almost always failing, to ride a surfboard with some grace. He had been trying that off and on since he was nine, and he didn't think he was really any better at it now.

His mother made the food she knew he liked: the Hungarian goulash she'd learned to make when his father had been stationed in Vienna, the marinated thick strip steaks that were always part of a trip home, the Western sandwiches before he went to bed.

Three times, they went out to dinner. Once to the home

of his mother's best friend, whose husband was also off at war. That had been awkward, with the women so carefully avoiding the subject of their husbands and the Army and the war, which Bill knew was all they really had to talk about. On Thursday they went to a restaurant in Honolulu for the Polynesian dinner that, like the steaks and the goulash, was traditional for them. On Saturday his mother asked if he'd like to go out to the club.

He didn't want to go to the club, but he smiled and said yes. There were other clubs in the area, but they both understood she meant the Schofield Barracks Officers' Open Mess. He had learned to swim at the pool there. It was like home.

When it was time to go, and he came out of his room wearing a civilian suit, she said, "Oh, Billy, I thought you'd wear your uniform."

The reply came automatically. "Why, Mother, how people would talk. The General's Lady out for the evening with a lowly warrant officer." The minute he said it he was sorry.

"I don't think that's at all funny," his mother said.

It was an awkward moment, but it passed. They were both aware it was his last night home. He offered a flimsy excuse: "I have to wear the tropical worsted tomorrow, and I only have one set."

"I'd forgotten," she said. "Your father has so many uniforms."

They got the car out of the garage. She made a further gesture.

"Would you like to drive, dear?"

"If you'd rather," he said, and got behind the wheel.

It was about twenty miles from Honolulu out to Schofield Barracks, and the trip took about forty minutes. The club parking lot was crowded. He decided to drop his mother off at the main door, and then park the car himself. An MP on duty, however, motioned him into a parking spot right beside the club, one of a dozen marked by neat white signs: "RESERVED FOR GENERAL OFFICERS."

He remembered then the military solution to the problem of general officers who lived in Hawaii, but were not connected with a base. Traditionally, officers assigned to one of the bases were given bumper stickers with the name of the installation and a number, with number one reserved for the commanding general and the numbers working higher as the rank went down. For officers who lived in Hawaii, and who were entitled to the privileges of their rank even if they weren't commanding anything there, a special bumper sticker was passed out, using stars and initials. On the front and rear bumpers of the car Bill was driving was a bumper sticker bearing two stars and the initials WCB. The MP had seen this, and motioned him into the special parking lot.

But when Bill got out of the car and started to walk toward the mess itself, the MP stopped him.

"Excuse me, sir," he said. "Whose car is that?"

"General Byrnes's," Bill said.

"Is the general with you, sir?"

"No," Bill said. "Mrs. Byrnes is. I'm the general's son."

"I see," the MP said, and smiled. "Thank you."

I'm not really the general's son, Bill thought. He's told me that himself. I should have parked that car about as far from the mess as I could get.

His mother was waiting inside the lobby. He put on a smile for her, and joked with her.

"How would the lovely lady like a cocktail before dinner?" he asked.

"The lovely lady would be delighted with a cocktail before dinner," she said, and took his arm. They went into the bar. The bartender knew her.

"Good evening, Mrs. Byrnes," he said. "Nice to see you again. What can I make you?"

"Manhattan, please," Bill's mother said.

"Beer for me, please," Bill said.

The bartender looked at him, and then, embarrassed, said, "I'm afraid I'll have to see your identification, sir."

"What for?"

"Are you twenty-one, sir?"

If I'd worn that uniform, he wouldn't have asked, Bill thought.

"Let me have a Coke," Bill said.

"I'm sorry," the bartender said. "I don't make the rules."

"It won't be long now, dear," his mother said, and patted his hand.

The food was good, and the waiters showed the deference the Army pays to the wives of its senior officers. Because she asked him to, Bill danced with his mother twice, and about ten-thirty they went home.

In his room, as he packed, the feeling of unreality left him. That was his uniform hanging up there, with the warrant officer's insignia and the pilot's wings. He couldn't have parked his own car in the reserved-for-generals space, but he could have gone to the officer's club as his own right.

When he was sure that his mother was asleep, he went out of his room and into the room his father used as an office. One wall was glass, looking out over the Pacific. Two of the walls were covered with books. On the third was the gun rack, a solid row of weapons, some cheap and simple like his first .22, some expensive and ornate like the German *Drilling* his father had had custom-made while in Europe.

The key to the gun rack was in the first drawer to the left, under a box of cleaning patches. It had always been there. He took it and went to the far end of the gun wall and unlocked a cabinet with a false-drawer front. This was the pistol cabinet, a neatly arranged display of hand guns. One gun was gone, the Colt .45 ACP New Service revolver. His grandfather had carried that gun, and his father was apparently now carrying it in Vietnam, as he'd carried it in Europe and Korea. A lot of cavalrymen preferred the revolver to the service automatic.

It was Warrant Officer Junior Grade Wilson C. Byrnes's professional judgment that his father was wrong. He liked the service automatic, providing, of course, that it had been accurized. He reached down and took his pistol from its felt and foam-rubber bed. He'd been given that gun at the age of fourteen. Irish Finnegan had had a friend who just happened to be an armorer and who just happened to have the spare time and spare parts to convert it from a standard Model 1911A1 .45 automatic into a National Match pistol. From a machine rest, it would put five bullets into an inch-and-a-half circle at fifty yards. The gun was capable of shooting far more accurately than Bill was, but since he was going to be a soldier, it was nice to know the gun he might have to use was accurate and reliable.

Bill pulled a chair up to the gun cabinet shelf, and then from another drawer took out a scrap of rug, used as long as he could remember to protect the finish of the cabinet while guns were being cleaned and worked on. Working with the speed of much practice, he stripped the gun down to its frame and carefully cleaned and oiled it. He was in the process of putting it back together when he became aware that his mother was in the room.

She was watching him.

"I thought you'd gone to bed," he said.

"I had trouble sleeping," she said. "And then I heard you in here. I thought you might not be able to find . . . what you were looking for."

"I'm taking this with me," he said.

"I thought you would," she said. And then she forced herself to change the subject. "How about a snack? A Western sandwich?"

"Love one," Bill said.

"I'll make it and take it out on the balcony," she said. "And we can watch the ocean while we eat."

When the pistol was reassembled, he put the cleaning materials back where they belonged, locked everything up, and went into his room. He wrapped the pistol in his underwear and put it where it would be hidden from anything but a detailed search. It was against regulations to carry your own guns to Vietnam, but Bill had decided he was just going to ignore that regulation. He didn't think that it would really be enforced. And what could they do if they did catch him? Send him to Vietnam?

He went out on the apartment balcony and ate his Western sandwich and drank a large glass of milk. Then he kissed his mother goodnight and went to bed.

At nine-thirty the next morning, he boarded a Boeing 707 which bore the colors of Northwest Orient Airlines. He waved at his mother, standing on the roof of the terminal building, but doubted if she saw him.

He felt sorry for his mother. She had spent most of her life saying good-bye to her men as they went off to war. Far better to be the wife of a bank teller or a mechanic. They got home every night, and if they were gone you didn't have to hold your breath every time the phone rang, afraid that it was Western Union, about to relay the regrets and sympathy of the Secretary of the Army.

As the jet began to move, Bill could see in his mind the takeoff: the slow lumbering along the runway, the incompletely burned JP–4 fuel pouring out the tail pipes of the engines, then the lift-off, and finally, when the pilot had flying speed, the nose-high attitude as the plane simultaneously gained altitude and picked up speed.

The passengers were almost all soldiers, airmen or sailors, including the inevitable half dozen would-be Romeos trying to make an impression on the stewardesses. But otherwise it was a civilian flight. There were magazines and in-flight movies and a fine meal served by a pretty girl with a toothpaste-ad smile. His seatmates were an Army technical sergeant, a Signal Corps radio expert, and a Navy lieutenant junior grade, who was a doctor en route to join the Marines.

The plane stopped for fuel at Tokyo International Airport, which Bill remembered as Tachikawa Air Force Base. He'd flown out of here before, too, as a dependent passenger. They took off again through a light rain.

Fourteen hours after leaving Honolulu, Bill felt the jet begin to sink. They were letting down. Because they'd picked up eight time zones and crossed the international date line, it was now four in the afternoon, and Sunday.

And then the gentle throttle noise of the jets diminished.

There was a chirp and the wheels touched. The engines revved as the pilot applied reverse thrust.

Out the windows they could see Vietnam. They were at the Tan Son Nhut airport, one of the busiest in the world. Civilian aircraft ranging from the latest jets, like theirs, to battered old Gooney Birds, DC–3's of Air America and Air Vietnam, shared the field with Air Force transports and fighters and Army helicopters and light cargo aircraft.

His first impression of Vietnam was to endure. As soon as the door opened and the hot, moist outside air came into the cabin, he thought, it's just like a steam bath.

The stewardesses gathered at the door to say good-bye, as they always do on airliners, but here there was a difference. The girls, as they smiled and shook hands, said, "Good luck." One little redhead looked as if she might be pretty close to tears.

There were guides, soldiers, waiting for them in the terminal, to show them where to collect their luggage and to direct them to waiting transportation. It took a bus and a truck to carry all the warrant officers junior grade and their luggage from the terminal building to the 17th Replacement Battalion on the other side of the field. Most of the men he already knew. They had been at Camp Wolters and Fort Rucker at the same time he'd been there. But there wasn't the intimacy here, the buddy-buddy business that he'd known at West Point, and for that matter while taking basic. The buddy-buddy business, he thought, as he considered this for the first time, had a teen-age hangout, collegiate air to it. They had buddied together because they weren't quite sure of themselves, because there seemed to be strength in numbers.

When you learned how to fly, you quickly matured. It was something you did on your own. You became a man the first moment you willed your hand to haul upward on the collective and move the bird into the air. You learned then what you were, and you didn't need anyone else's approval.

There were, of course, vestigial remnants of the college classroom and the enlisted barracks. There were handshakes and backslapping and jokes:

"Sergeant," one of them said, "where do I go to tell the man I've changed my mind?"

"The man'll be here in a minute, mister," the sergeant said, tolerantly. It certainly wasn't the first time he'd heard that line, or others like it.

The Man was a little gray-haired major of the Adjutant General's Corps, and he had expected them.

"On behalf of the Commander-in-Chief, Mac Vee," he said, "gentlemen, welcome to the Republic of Vietnam."

Behind him, someone whispered, "What's Mac Vee?"

"Military Assistance Command, Vietnam," someone else whispered.

"There will be a formal briefing first thing in the morning," the major went on. "Tonight, you are restricted to the area. After the briefing, you will be given your assignments here. There's an officers' club, and a movie, and there's a map outside this building to show you where they are. I've got one unpleasant thing to remind you of. Leaving the area here will not be considered simply absence without leave. It will be regarded as absence without leave to avoid hazardous duty, and dealt with accordingly. Our job here is to get you through the in-processing as quickly as possible, and to your units. As you're probably aware, there is a pilot shortage, and you are therefore priority material. Don't mess us up, and we'll do our best to make your stay as pleasant — and as brief — as possible. That's all, gentlemen, we'll see you in the morning."

Someone called attention, and they got to their feet and the major walked out of the room.

He was as good as his word. Just after lunch the next day, Bill and eight others from the pool of replacement warrant officer pilots were trucked out to a De Havilland Otter, the largest airplane in the world powered by just one engine.

Warrant Officer Junior Grade Wilson Campbell Byrnes III had been relieved of assignment 17th Replacement Battalion and was transferred to and would proceed by Military Air Transportation to the 170th Aviation Company, 52d Combat Aviation Battalion, APO 96267 (Pleiku).

Once they were airborne and out of the humidity of the airfield, which was just about at sea level, it was a pleasant flight. From the air, Vietnam was a beautiful country, lush and green with gently rolling hills and an intricate pattern of roads and waterways and rice paddies.

At ten minutes past five, the Otter pilot began to let down in a steep descent right over the Pleiku airfield. As they got closer to the ground, they could see the perimeter defense of the field: the serpentine coils of barbed wire, called concertina, the high observation towers, and the raw earth of the entrenchments. The field itself was covered with aircraft, both Air Force and Army, each in its own little earthwork or sandbag revetment. Each building was similarly protected by an earthwork of some kind.

They touched down finally and taxied to Base Operations. Here they were met by a captain and a handful of enlisted men who helped them load their baggage onto a three-quarter-ton truck, and then drove them across the field to the 170th Combat Aviation Company headquarters building.

There the commanding officer, a young-faced but already balding major wearing jungle fatigues of mottled camouflage cotton, waited for them. They were called to attention, put at ease, and he walked down the little field of men, shaking each one's hand and asking their names.

"I'm Major Harrison Kramer," he said. "People around here call me 'Dutch' or 'the Old Man' but not to my face. I think this is the largest aviation company in Vietnam. I *know* it's the best aviation company in Vietnam. We're glad to have you, of course, but you should consider this a good assignment. We're a reinforced company: that is, we have a large and versatile platoon of gunships. Some are armed with eight machine guns, some with machine guns and rockets, some with just a couple of guns and a lot of rockets. We tailor the ordnance to suit the mission, in other words. All of our slicks, the cargo ships, have a door gun on both sides. There are two platoons of slicks, *plus* a service platoon flying everything from H–13 Bells to a Skycrane on loan from the First Cavalry. We've *also* got four Chinooks. The reason we're reinforced and have all the odd aircraft is that we're called upon to do practically anything anyone ever thought to do with a helicopter. You may not look back fondly on your assignment here, but I can promise you won't look back and remember you were bored.

"I'll see that you're given some place to live, and shown the mess. In the morning, we'll start checking you out. At that time, you can give your check pilot your preference of

26

assignment. Except, of course, that we're not accepting volunteers to fly the Crane. The First Cav send their own people to fly that."

The officers of the 170th Aviation Company were billeted in tents. It wasn't as crude, nor as uncomfortable, as it might sound. First, the tents had wooden frames and floors. The walls of the tent were rolled up, exposing the inside to any wind that might get past the plastic netting nailed to the tent frame and the wall of sandbags surrounding the tent. There were electric lights, beds, mattresses, sheets, more mosquito netting, shelves, lockers and a telephone. In the center of each tent were wooden tables. In effect, each of the six men in the tent had his own private cubicle.

At one end of each row of tents was a latrine, and at the opposite end a wash tent, complete with shower. There were paths of white sand bordered with rocks. Except that it was obviously more practical and comfortable, it reminded Bill Byrnes of a summer camp he'd once attended.

They were taken to a supply tent where they each drew sheets for their beds, a bag for dirty laundry, four sets of jungle fatigues, a steel helmet and other field equipment, and a .38 Special Smith and Wesson revolver.

"Sergeant," Bill said in a low voice, so the others wouldn't hear him, "I've got a pistol."

"What have you got?"

"National Match .45."

"Can you use it?" the sergeant asked.

"Yes," Bill said, simply.

"You're not supposed to have your own, Mr. Byrnes," the sergeant said. "You're supposed to carry this thing. But if you noticed, the Old Man's carrying a National Match

.45, too. Why don't you check with him in the morning? Take this now, and you can always turn it in."

"Thank you," Bill said.

He didn't have to wait until morning. He had just finished making his bed and was bending over his canvas suitcase to start unpacking when he heard the door of his tent creak open. It was Major Kramer, "the Old Man." Bill stood to attention. None of his new tentmates were in the tent yet.

"At ease, Byrnes," Major Kramer said. "I won you in the lottery and I thought I'd come get acquainted. Have you eaten yet?"

"No, sir, I was just unpacking. What's the lottery, sir?"

"There are three instruction pilots besides me," Kramer said, sitting down on a folding wooden chair. "There are seven of you. Check ride takes half the morning. We've got an afternoon mission. That means one of you was left over. The IP's went Eeeny Meeny Miney Moe and I got you."

"Oh," Bill said.

"You don't seem worried," the major said.

"I think I can pass the check ride," Bill said. "If that's what you mean."

"How old are you, Byrnes?"

"Nineteen."

"How many hours?"

"Just over three hundred fifty."

"You think you're a hotshot pilot?" the major asked.

"I didn't say that," Bill said. "I said I think I can pass a check ride."

"Where are you from?"

"My family lives in Hawaii," Bill said.

"I'm from Texas. If Texans are as mean as people say, and if Germans are too, that makes me twice mean. My family moved from Braunfels, Germany, to a place in Texas they named New Braunfels. I went to A and M. I'm an Aggie."

"I didn't go to college. Or anyway I didn't finish the year," Bill said.

"You've got time to go back," Kramer said. "What do you want to be?"

"A marine biologist," Bill said.

"That's a fisherman who gets paid for it, right?"

"I guess so," Bill said, and chuckled. "I never thought of it that way." He had come to the underwear-wrapped .45 in his bag. He turned and faced Major Kramer.

"Sir, I've got a little problem."

"Already? You just got here."

"I've got a .45," Bill said.

"You're not supposed to have a .45. Somebody sell it to you at the Replacement Battalion?"

"No, sir, I brought it with me."

"You got it there?" the major asked. Then, without waiting for an answer, "Let me see it."

Bill took the clip from the pistol, and then opened the action before handing it over. Major Kramer peered inside the open action to double-check that it wasn't loaded, and then let the action slide forward. He pointed it at the floor and gently squeezed the trigger until it clicked. Then he cocked the hammer and dry-fired it again.

"Nice trigger," he said. "Can you use it?"

"I can use part of it," Bill said. "I'm not that good a shot."

"Let's go see," Major Kramer said.

"Sir?"

"You have the rest of the night to unpack, and the mess closes in forty-five minutes. We'll go see if you can shoot this thing, and get something to eat."

"Yes, sir," Bill said.

Major Kramer handed Bill the pistol, and then walked out of the tent. Bill followed him, almost trotting to keep up with him. Kramer led him to another tent, in which a young captain was standing.

"Captain Hawker, Mr. Byrnes," Major Kramer said. "He's one of the new ones."

Hawker walked across the tent and shook hands. "Glad to know you," he said. Then he saw the pistol. "Oh, don't tell me you're another cannon shooter. One in the company is enough."

"He's a cannon owner," Major Kramer said. "We're about to find out if he's a cannon shooter." He slid a heavy Army safe from under his bed and worked the combination. When he pulled the door open, he took out two 50-round boxes of pistol ammunition. "You want to go with us, Hawk? Have you eaten?"

"I'll go," Captain Hawker said.

The three of them walked down the sand walkway to the end of the row of tents, and then across an open area to the barbed-wire fence surrounding the camp. Suddenly Major Kramer raised his voice.

"Sentry!"

"Here, sir," a soldier said, standing up inside a sandbag-protected shanty. He was carrying an AR–15 automatic rifle.

"We're going to fire a few rounds. Get on the horn and

tell the Sergeant of the Guard not to have kittens," Major Kramer said.

"Yes, sir," the sentry said, and smiled.

Along the protective line of concertina were wooden poles three inches thick, to which the coils of barbed wire were nailed. Major Kramer walked to the sentry's hut and reached into a box which was apparently full of empty condensed-milk cans. He picked up a handful. Then, by stepping carefully and stretching, he was able to set five cans on the poles without catching himself in the barbed wire.

He came back to where Bill and Captain Hawker stood and handed Bill a box of ammunition.

"The flag is up, the flag is waving, the flag is down," he said, mimicking the standard firing-range orders. "Commence firing."

"There's no backdrop," Bill protested.

"And there's nobody out there but Charlie," Major Kramer said. "A fact which I suggest you tattoo on your forehead so you don't forget it."

"You mean the enemy? Why do they call him Charlie?" Bill asked.

"From the phonetics," Kramer replied. "V.C. equals Victor Charlie. Shortened to Charlie."

Bill was a little embarrassed. He should have been able to figure that out himself.

"Go ahead, Byrnes. You say you can shoot that thing. Let's see you."

Bill loaded five of the squat, shiny cartridges into the pistol's magazine, and then shoved the magazine into the butt of the .45. He pointed the pistol at the ground and worked the action. The gun was now loaded and ready to fire.

He looked at Major Kramer, who was watching him impatiently. Bill raised the pistol, lined up the sights and fired at one of the shiny condensed-milk cans. He missed.

"You missed," Major Kramer said, quite unnecessarily. Bill was suddenly furious with himself. He hadn't been at Pleiku two hours and he was already about to make a fool of himself.

He lined up the sights again and fired again, and this time the can went sailing off into the air. Bill looked at Major Kramer.

"I guess he wants a medal, Hawk," Major Kramer said.

Furious again, Bill lined up the sights on another can and squeezed the trigger. The can went sailing. He fired twice again, each time hitting a can. Then he looked at Major Kramer again.

"Okay," the major said. "You can shoot it. Four out of five isn't luck." Then he picked up two more of the cans. He tossed them to Captain Hawker, then drew his own pistol and worked the action. "Go," he said. Hawker threw a milk can in the air. Kramer fired at it and missed. But before it touched the ground, he fired again and hit it. Then he looked at Hawker again. "Go," he said, and Hawker threw the other can. This time, Kramer hit it twice before it touched the ground.

He unloaded the gun's chamber, filled the clip from the box of ammunition he'd given Bill, and then he said. "That was an exhibition of the military art known as impressing the troops."

"I'm impressed," Bill said. Kramer smiled.

"I'll tell you what, Byrnes," he said, still smiling. "You can carry that .45, and no questions asked. I always give newly arrived officers one pardon for breaking standing orders. That's yours." He was still smiling, but Bill understood that he was by no means joking.

"Yes, sir," he said. "Thank you, sir."

"Let's go eat, gentlemen," Major Kramer said, holstering his pistol. Bill had no holster. There was nothing he could do with the pistol except stick it in his hip pocket. He put it there, and walked down the sand path after the Old Man.

## ✤ 3 ✤

THERE WAS someone shaking him gently when he woke up. The tent was still dark, but there was a flashlight in his face.

"Mr. Byrnes?" the voice asked.

"Yeah," he said.

"The Old Man asked me to give you this before breakfast, sir," the face said.

"Who're you?"

"I'm Sergeant Santos," the face said. "I crew the major's Huey."

"What is it?" Bill said, awake now, sitting up in bed.

"A holster and a couple of magazine pouches for your pistol," the sergeant said. "You better be getting up, Mr. Byrnes," he added.

"What time is it?"

"A few minutes to five, and the major likes to be off the ground by six."

"He told me after breakfast," Bill protested.

"If I was you, Mr. Byrnes," Sergeant Santos said. "I'd be on the flight line at ten minutes to six."

"I'll be there, Sergeant," Bill said. "Thank you."

He got up and dressed quickly in his flight suit of blue-gray coveralls, strapped the web belt and the .45 around his waist, and hurried to the mess, where he gulped his breakfast. He was on the flight line at quarter of six, and Major Kramer was nowhere in sight. At ten of six, however, he showed up, with Sergeant Santos and another enlisted man tailing behind him.

"Are you nervous, Byrnes?" he asked. "Or did Santos here warn you that I like to be off the ground by six?"

"Thank you for the holster, sir," Bill said, unwilling to answer the two questions asked.

"This is Specialist Cohen," Kramer said. "He's a dropout from the First Division."

"Pleased tameetcha, sir," Cohen said, identifying himself as a New Yorker with that one sentence.

"How are you, Cohen?" Bill said. They shook hands, somewhat awkwardly — Cohen had a machine gun cradled in his right arm.

"How's the bird, Santos? Is that wreck of yours flyable?" Major Kramer asked.

"That bird'll be flying when they put the last of these in the Smithsonian," Santos said.

"Your aircraft is Four Double-O Two, Mr. Byrnes," Major Kramer said. "Sergeant Santos is the crew chief, and he will help you with the preflight. I'll take care of filing the flight plan."

"Yes, sir."

"Over this way, Mr. Byrnes," Santos said. He led Bill to a Bell HU–1D helicopter, a Huey. Bill began to make the preflight inspection, wholly aware that Kramer would ask Santos how well he did this, whether he was thorough or sloppy, careful or careless. He gave the machine a very careful preflight inspection. He was for a moment confused by what appeared to be several small hatches in the aircraft skin. Then he realized they weren't hatches at all, but patches where something, a bullet, for example, had broken the skin.

"Seems to have been shot up," he said.

"One hundred thirty-two perforations," Santos said, rather proudly. "We've made six forced landings due to enemy action."

"Didn't they teach you how to duck?" Bill asked. Santos smiled at him.

"This is a good ol' bird," Santos said.

"I'm not used to having a crew along for a check ride," Bill said.

"Well, I won't say I'm overjoyed, Mr. Byrnes," Santos said. "Like I could have slept this morning. But a crew is a good thing to have along in case you get zapped by Charlie."

"I guess it is," Bill said. "And I suppose Major Kramer is known for giving rough check rides?"

"The roughest," Santos agreed.

"Don't blow your cool, Mr. Byrnes," Cohen offered helpfully. "The Old Man is Number One."

"He's all right," Santos said, in agreement. By the way he said it, Bill realized that it was a first-class, unqualified compliment.

"Is it all here, Mr. Byrnes?" Major Kramer asked, walking up and handing him the flight plan on a clipboard.

"Yes, sir," Bill said. "Preflight completed, sir."

"Santos?" Major Kramer asked.

"It's okay, Major," Santos said. Bill understood that the major had asked whether his preflight inspection had been conducted properly, rather than if the aircraft itself were safe to fly.

"You drive, Mr. Byrnes," Major Kramer said. "Cohen, you ready?"

"Yes, sir."

Bill went to the right side of the Huey and climbed into the pilot's seat. He made a tentative stab at the directional control pedals with his feet and then reached down and unfastened the seat lock so that he could slide the seat forward. Then he fastened his seat and shoulder harnesses and plugged in the cord dangling from the side of his hard hat. He reached out and turned on the MASTER COMMO switch. There was a whining noise behind him in the radio compartment, and the slight buzzing in his earphones told him the system was working.

He reached up over his head for the checklist, a plastic-covered white card tied to the sun visor with a length of key chain. He handed it to Major Kramer as soon as Kramer had strapped himself in his seat.

"Any time, Major," Bill said.

"Collective Pitch," the major's voice came over the intercom. "Down and locked," Bill replied.

"Throttle," the major said. Bill answered, "Closed."

"Ignition System." . . . "In."

"Starter Circuit Breaker." . . . "In."

"Inverter Switch." . . . "Main."

"Battery." . . . "On."

"Starter Generator." . . . "Set."

"Main Generator." . . . "On."

"Fuel Warning Light." . . . "Check," Bill said, as he reached forward and pushed the push-to-test light and it came on.

"Fuel Gauge," the major said, and Bill replied, "Check."

"Caution Panel Warning Light." . . . "Check."

"Throttle." . . . "Fully closed."

"Cyclic Control," the major read. Bill moved the control stick between his legs in a small circle to see that it was free and then centered it before saying, "Centered."

"Fire Guard," Kramer's voice said metallically. Bill looked out the window and saw Santos standing with a fire extinguisher at the ready. "Posted," Bill said.

"Rotor Blades," Kramer called, and Bill shouted, "Clear," and then gestured to Santos that they were about to start up by holding his right index finger above his head and making a whirling motion. Santos nodded.

"Battery." . . . "On."

"Fuel Main Switch." . . . "On."

"Oil Valve." . . . "On."

"Fuel Start Switch." . . . "On."

"Governor." . . . "On."

"Throttle." . . . "Ground idle."

"RPM Control." . . . "Minimum."

"Starter Ignition Switch," Major Kramer read, and Bill replied, "Pulling on it."

There was a whine and a vibration, a whistling that grew and a vibration that grew and then suddenly smoothed out. The engine caught. The rotor blade began very slowly to turn. Bill glanced at the instrument panel. No fire-warning lights came on. He gestured with his hand for Santos to get aboard. Santos nodded, and disappeared from sight. There was a click in the earphones as Santos plugged his helmet in. "Crew chief aboard, sir," his voice said.

Bill looked down at the control panel in front of him, a rather impressive array of instruments that he had once looked at with a sinking feeling in his stomach, certain that he would never be able to remember what all the gauges and indicators stood for, much less what they were supposed to read. But now they were as familiar to him, and as easy to read, as the face of his watch.

Just to the left of the center of the control panel were six round dials, in two columns of three. The top two dials gave the fuel pressure and the quantity of fuel. The two immediately beneath them gave the engine oil pressure and temperature. The lowest two were the transmission oil pressure and temperature. Four other dials below these told the load on the main generator and the standby generator, and the amount of AC and DC voltage being used.

Directly in front of Bill were four instruments arranged horizontally. The one on the left was the Tachometer, which had two indicator needles, one giving engine rpm and the other rotor revolutions per minute. Next to this was the Airspeed Indicator. The largest and most complicated instrument in the helicopter came next, the Attitude Indicator. This was connected to an elaborate system of gyroscopes and computers in the radio compartment, and showed a ball, with its top half white and its bottom half black. A little gull-shaped wing marker on the instrument represented the helicopter. When the wing appeared to be just on the line between the white (the sky) and the black (the earth) the ship would be flying straight and level. If it appeared to dip into the black, the helicopter would be descending, in the white, climbing. If it looked tilted, the helicopter was in a bank.

Bill's advanced flight instructor had described the Attitude Indicator to him very simply: "It's like taking a little bit of the earth with you. That ball never moves. You and the helicopter move around it. And if you think you're having a hard time learning how to fly, consider how it was for pilots before they thought up that little gadget."

Beside the Attitude Indicator was the Altimeter. Directly below that was the Vertical Velocity Indicator, which told you how fast you were going up or down. The trouble with both of these instruments, particularly in a helicopter, was that they told you how high you were and how fast you were falling, several seconds ago — as many as seven seconds — and you traveled a great distance in seven seconds.

Immediately below the Attitude Indicator were the Radio Compass dials. This instrument was connected to radios in the radio compartment and showed, on two needles, the directions of two stations at any one time. By tuning in a radio station on the ground, and by flying the helicopter so that the needle of the instrument pointed to the top of the dial, you could fly to that station. You could also find out where you were by tuning into two different stations whose locations were known, seeing where the needles pointed, and then drawing lines from them on a map. Where the lines joined was your position.

Below the Radio Compass was the Omni Indicator, a more sophisticated version of the Radio Compass, which used a special ground radio, an omnidirectional radio transmitter, to provide navigation information. To the left of the Omni Indicator was the Turn and Slip Indicator, a needle and ball which showed aircraft attitude.

Below the Tachometer were three dials in a column. The first gave the pounds of torque being applied by the engine to the transmission; the second gave the revolutions of the jet engines' gas producer, and the third gave the exhaust temperature, a guide to the efficiency of the engine.

All these instruments had once baffled Bill with their complexity. But now they were all familiar; in fact, the interior of the helicopter was the most familiar thing he'd yet found in Vietnam.

"The tower is Tiger-Lily," Major Kramer told him over the earphones.

"Roger. Thank you," Bill said. His eyes went back and forth over the instrument panel. One by one, the indicator needles moved so that their points touched little strips of green painted on their faces to show safe and proper temperatures and pressures.

Finally, he pushed the intercom button on his cyclic control stick and said, "All in the green. Permission to take off, sir?"

"Roger. Go ahead," Major Kramer said.

"Ready back there?" Bill asked, and Cohen and Santos replied, "Yes, sir."

"Tiger-Lily, this is Four Double-O Two in front of Base Ops," Bill said, pulling the two-position switch on the cyclic all the way back, so that his microphone was now connected to the transmitter rather than the intercom.

"Go ahead, Double-O Two."

"Double-O Two to the active for takeoff."

"Double-O Two is cleared to the active, to hold on the threshold," the tower replied. "The time is zero five past the hour. The winds are negligible. The altimeter is two niner-niner."

Bill activated the intercom. "Ready in the back seat?"

"Ready, sir," the two men in the back answered, their voices over one another. Bill looked at the major.

"Ready, sir?"

"Let's go, Mr. Byrnes," Major Kramer said.

Bill's eyes ran across the instrument panel quickly. Everything was in the green. He slowly pulled up on the collective pitch control with his right hand. The Huey trembled, and they lifted an inch or so, and then four and then six inches off the ground. Bill moved the cyclic forward so slightly that it would have taken another pilot to detect the movement. The nose of the Huey dropped, the movement barely perceptible. But the helicopter was flying, and they were moving. He moved it forward very slowly, at about a walking pace, until he was on the threshold of the runway.

Then he pulled the radio transmit switch. "Double-O Two holding on the threshold."

"Clear to go, Double-O Two."

"Roger," Bill said. He dropped the nose of the Huey and at the same time hauled up slightly on the collective. The Huey rose four or five feet in the air and then began to move ever more quickly down the runway. "Double-O Two off the deck at six past the hour," Bill said through his microphone.

The airspeed indicator sprang to life as they passed forty knots, and then began to climb. When they were making seventy knots, Bill hauled up more on the collective, and the Huey soared into the air. This was the part of helicopter flying that he liked best, when you could soar like a bird.

Suddenly, the helicopter stopped soaring and began to sink rapidly. He'd lost power. He took a quick look at the tachometer, and made an immediate autorotation to the ground, to his right.

An autorotation at a low altitude is perhaps the most difficult of all helicopter flying maneuvers. It requires skill and fine coordination. Essentially, it's a question of swapping inertia for energy. As you can use the power of the engine to turn the rotor blades and thus get lift, you can reverse the process around, turning the rotor blades by the inertia of the falling machine. At the last possible moment, as the helicopter nears the ground, the process is reversed again, using the inertia of the rotating blades themselves to gain a few seconds of lift, enough to flare out and to settle the machine on the ground.

Bill had fully expected that Major Kramer would give him an autorotation as part of the check ride. But he had assumed that Kramer would wait until he had some small idea of his skill before cutting the engine. So apparently, had the control tower.

"Double-O Two, are you in trouble?"

"Negative," Kramer said. "Just an autorotation. Thanks just the same."

They were sitting on the runway. The engine was running again. "I didn't expect that," Bill said.

"You never expect an engine failure," Kramer said. "But that's not bad for openers, Mr. Byrnes."

"You ready to go, sir?"

"Any time."

"Double-O Two light on the skids," Bill told the tower.

"You're clear, Double-O Two," the tower said. Bill made another takeoff, and this time Major Kramer allowed him to climb to about 3,500 feet, outside the range of most small-arms fire. Then he gave him a check ride that started with the simplest maneuvers he'd learned at Camp Wolters and ended with the most complicated flying he'd learned at Fort Rucker.

Afterwards, the major took over the controls and demonstrated some things that had a special Vietnam application. He showed, for example, how to give the gunner in the rear a stable platform from which to machine-gun the ground, and how to make the helicopter a smaller, harder-to-hit target for Viet Cong ground fire. After he'd demonstrated the maneuvers, he watched while Bill tried them himself.

Finally, he said, "That's about it, I think, Mr. Byrnes. Take us home, and we'll introduce you to your aircraft commander. We're flying an assault this afternoon."

When they were back on the ground, sitting in front of Base Operations, and Bill had helped Sergeant Santos and Specialist Cohen tie the helicopter down, Major Kramer draped an arm around Santos's shoulders.

"Well, what do you think, Sergeant?"

"He's a lot better than some of them we've got lately, Major," Santos said, professionally.

"Remember that long lanky guy? The one who lost his cool?" Cohen asked.

"Let us say," Major Kramer said, "that he did not demonstrate Mr. Byrnes's prompt reaction to the loss of power on takeoff."

"What happened?" Bill asked.

"We bent it up, Mr. Byrnes," Cohen said. "Scratch one bird."

"Oh," Bill said.

"We ought to light up about quarter after one," Kramer said to Santos.

"Thirteen-fifteen," Santos said. "Yes, sir."

"Come along, Mr. Byrnes," Major Kramer said, "and meet your new boss."

Warrant Officer Junior Grade Byrnes's new boss turned out to be a stocky, square-faced young lieutenant with hair

44

cut so short that it looked for a moment as if it had been shaved. Even before he saw the ring on his finger Bill sensed that he was a West Pointer.

"Morning, Hal," Kramer said.

"Good morning, sir." They did not exchange salutes, but the lieutenant came to a position that was pretty close to attention.

"Lieutenant Halverson. Mr. Byrnes. Mr. Byrnes will be your co-pilot this afternoon."

Bill saluted before he extended his hand. Halverson said, very formally and with a stiff smile, "How do you do, Mr. Byrnes? I'm very glad to know you."

"How do you do, sir?" Bill replied.

"Just graduated, did you?"

"Yes, sir."

"Has he had his check ride?" Halverson asked.

"Just came in from it," Kramer said.

"May I ask, sir, with whom he rode?"

"With me, Lieutenant," Kramer said.

"In that case, that's fine, then," Halverson said.

"Thank you very much, Lieutenant," Kramer said, "for respecting my judgment." There was no mistaking the sarcasm. "Briefing's at twelve. I'll see you at Base Ops then," Kramer said, and walked away. He didn't give either of them a chance to come to attention or salute. One second he was talking and the next he was walking away.

Halverson examined Bill closely. It was a familiar type of examination. Bill had been looked at that way by upperclassmen in his time in Beast Barracks at West Point. He didn't like it at all.

"I don't suppose you've had much service, have you?" Halverson asked.

"No, sir, not very much."

"Would you mind telling me how much?"

"About ten months, sir," Bill said.

"How many hours do you have?"

"About three hundred fifty, sir," Bill said.

"I didn't ask for an approximation, mister, I asked how many hours."

"Three hundred fifty-six, plus what I flew this morning, sir."

"There's no place here for someone who is sloppy, Mr. Byrnes," Halverson said. "The sooner you fully appreciate that, the better."

"Yes, sir."

"The authorized sidearm for aircraft pilots is the .38 Special Smith and Wesson revolver, Mr. Byrnes," Halverson said. "How is it that you're carrying an unauthorized weapon?"

"Sir, I have the Major's permission to carry the .45."

"I'll check on that, Mr. Byrnes," Halverson said. The implication was clear that he didn't trust Bill.

"Yes, sir."

"That'll be all for the moment, Mr. Byrnes," Halverson said. "I'll see you in the briefing room at eleven forty-five."

"Yes, sir. Thank you, sir," Bill said, and came to attention and saluted.

Halverson's salute in return was snappy and precise. Bill about-faced and started to walk off.

"Just a moment, Mr. Byrnes," Halverson said. "I think I should say I appreciate your military bearing and courtesy. We don't often get that in new warrant officers. Did you, by chance, take ROTC in college?"

"No, sir, I did not take ROTC in college," Bill said.

"Well, keep up the good work," Halverson said, and then exchanged salutes again.

"Yes, sir. Thank you, sir," Bill said.

I learned to play soldier the same place you did, you stuffy little jerk, Bill thought.

When he got to the tent, for the first time his tentmates were there and awake. There were four other warrant officers and a lieutenant. The lieutenant introduced himself first, and then the others.

"You going along this afternoon?" the lieutenant, whose name was Philips, asked.

"Yes, sir."

"They tell you who with?"

"Lieutenant Halverson, sir."

"Every unit is supposed to have one of those," one of the warrants said. "And Halverson, otherwise known as Baron von Beethoven, is ours. Tough luck, Byrnes."

It was the sort of remark that should have been corrected by the lieutenant. Warrant officers are not supposed to crack wise about commissioned officers. But the lieutenant said only, "Lieutenant Halverson is fond of classical music, Byrnes."

"And they call him the Baron because he thinks this is the Prussian Army," the warrant said.

"He's a good officer, Charley," the lieutenant said.

"So was Rommel," the warrant officer pilot named Charley said. "But I don't think I would have liked working for him, either."

"Let's go get early chow," said the lieutenant. "Briefing's at noon, and if we don't eat now, we go hungry."

The others started out the door. Lieutenant Philips laid a hand on Bill's arm, telling him to wait.

"Halverson is all right, Byrnes," he said. "He goes by the book. Maybe a little too much. But he's a West Pointer, and that's the way they play the game, I guess. He's liable to jump all over you for that .45 . . . Take that as a friendly word of advice."

"I've got permission to carry it," Bill said. "But thanks."

"You're going to have a tough row to hoe with that guy," Philips said. "If he leans a little too hard, whatever you do, don't tell him off. Tell me, and I'll lean a little the other way. It burns him up, but I happen to outrank him."

"I think I can get along with him all right, sir," Bill said, thinking: I know how to play his game. "But thanks, I appreciate that."

"I'm not a good guy," Philips said. "It's just that pilots are in such short supply that we can't afford to have any of them restricted to quarters waiting to be court-martialed for insubordination."

"I know how to keep my mouth shut, Lieutenant," Bill said.

"Atta boy," Philips said. "Now let's go chow up."

# ❋ 4 ❋

THE BRIEFING was conducted in a crude, corrugated steel walled and roofed building that apparently doubled as a movie theater at night. A projection screen hung from the ceiling.

Lieutenant Halverson was waiting at the door when Bill walked up with his tentmates. He saluted Philips, who returned it casually. "Hello, Hal," he said.

"Why don't you sit with me, Mr. Byrnes?" Halverson asked, but there was no mistaking the tone of voice for a suggestion. It was an order. Halverson led Bill to a bench in the front of the crude auditorium. The others hung to the back, reminding Bill of church, where the latecomers seemed to get stuck with the seats in front.

Promptly at twelve, Major Kramer, Captain Hawker and a roly-poly captain whom Bill hadn't seen before came in the side door. Everyone stood up.

"Take your seats," Major Kramer ordered even before he'd pulled the door closed behind him. He sat in a chair placed directly in the center of the aisle in the front row. It was battered and worn, but it was the only armchair in the room. On the back someone with a sense of humor had painted in fluorescent "Day-Glo" paint the word: HIS.

"OK, Hawke," Kramer said. "Let's get on with it."

"I didn't think you'd think to bring a notebook," Lieu-

49

tenant Halverson said quietly in Bill's ear. "So I brought one for you. In the future, see to it that you have one."

"Yes, sir," Bill said. "Thank you, sir."

He felt like a thirteen-year-old at military school, being scolded.

"Intelligence reports that a Charlie force estimated to be of reinforced company strength has been sighted in this general area," Hawker began, pointing at a map with a three-foot ruler. "A long-range reconnaissance platoon of the First Division — the Big Red One — has been in the area for the last couple of days, with only minor contact, although it is their opinion — it's that Indian sergeant from Oklahoma, I understand, and he's generally pretty good at it — that the intelligence report is accurate.

"In any event, we're going to lift in a battalion of the Eighteenth Infantry, augmented by some 105's. The Chinooks will lift the guns in a simultaneous move with the first assault wave of the troops. Now watch out for them. A Chinook hauling a cannon is hardly an H–13, which means you'll have to get out of their way, not the other way around.

"They'll place their cannon here and here and here and here," Hawker said, pointing with the ruler. "The whole idea of course is, if Charlie is in there, to force him to withdraw in this general direction. We already have the big stuff laid on to shell that area, to saturate that area. Now, it looks appealing, because it's flat and open. But if you have to sit down, don't sit down there. Not only is Charlie coming out that way, but that's where the artillery will be coming down.

"We will pick up the troops here," he said, pointing, "climb to fifty-five hundred feet, and orbit here." He pointed again. "We will make two deliveries of troops and then proceed to the staging area here, where, depending on how things go, we will be available for either dustoff or re-supply of ammo. The staging area will have our resupply of fuel. It will also be the fuel point for our Chinooks, and they have priority, so don't go scooting in ahead of them. And I don't think I should have to tell you . . . but I will . . . if a gunship shows up, we give him the benefit of the doubt and let him have first crack at the JP–4. Any questions so far?"

The map was marked with symbols that were easy to recognize. The Dustoffs — the Medical Evacuation helicopters — were represented by a silhouette of a Huey marked with a red cross. The huge twin-rotor supply choppers, the Chinooks, had their own silhouette symbols: cannons to identify the artillery. There were gas pumps to show the fueling area, and so on. It was a good, clean presentation.

Captain Hawker looked around the room, but no one seemed to have any questions.

"Aircraft commanders will come forward for radio call signs and frequencies," Hawker said. "The rest of you go to the flight line and start your preflights. Unless you have something, Major Kramer?"

Kramer stood up, and then leaned against his armchair.

"There was entirely too much juvenile radio chatter the last time," he said. "And since appeals to you as pilots and officers seem to fall on deaf ears, I'll try something else. Anyone I hear running off at the mouth over the air will, when he gets back here, write, 'I will close my fat yap,' one thousand times. Is that clearly understood?"

There were chuckles and a couple of loud snorts.

"And I am now making the standard speech. All aircraft

commanders will remind their gunners that the effective range of the machine gun is not five miles, and that every time it goes bang it costs the taxpayer two bits. In other words, I don't want them firing unless they've got a target, and then not unless they're within range." He looked around the room. "And a final word. I would much rather have you all here alive than the memory of you as dead heroes. In other words, watch yourselves. The Chaplain is presently holding forth in the chapel. I suggest that it would be a good idea if you routed yourselves over that way en route to the flight line. That's all, gentlemen. We'll fire up at thirteen-fifteen."

At Bill's side, Lieutenant Halverson called, "At-ten-hut!" and everyone in the room came to attention until Major Kramer had left the building.

When Bill got to the helicopter, a sergeant, obviously the crew chief, who had been sitting on the floor of the rear section with his feet dangling over the edge, slid off and walked up to him. He didn't salute.

"Are you the co-pilot?" he asked. Bill nodded. "It's ready to go," he said. "I preflighted it."

"Since I'm going along for the ride," Bill replied, "you won't mind, Sergeant, will you, if I preflight it myself?"

"No, sir," the sergeant said.

"Where's the door gunner?"

"We flipped to see who would get the ammo," the sergeant said. "He lost."

By the time Bill had completed his outside preflight inspection of the helicopter, the door gunner had appeared, riding in the back of a jeep driven by a broad-shouldered Negro master sergeant. The sergeant turned off the jeep engine and got out. He walked over to Bill and saluted.

"Mr. Byrnes?"

"Yep," Bill said.

"I'm Sergeant Gowald," he said. "I'm the armorer."

"How are you, Sergeant?" Bill said.

"I'm an old buddy of Irish Finnegan, Mr. Byrnes," Sergeant Gowald said. "You need anything, you just let me know. Irish wrote and told me to look you up."

"Thank you, Sergeant," Bill said, and smiled, and he thought that if he had Finnegan here, he'd pull rank on him and have him run around the field at port arms. He meant well, of course, but if Finnegan had written at all, it was more than likely that he had described Bill as "General Byrnes's kid."

"Irish and me was in Korea together," Gowald went on. "We know a lot of the same people."

"I'll bet," Bill said. Gowald had just as much as told him he knew about Bill's father.

"One thing about Irish," Gowald went on. "For an Irishman, he sure knows how to keep his mouth shut." He smiled, just a shade of a smile. He was not the broad-smiling type.

"Are we talking about the same guy?" Bill asked.

"Yes, sir," Gowald said. "Same guy."

"Who are you talking about?" the crew chief asked.

"Some sergeant Mr. Byrnes knew before he got to be a warrant," Gowald said. "Well, nice to see you, Mr. Byrnes. I'll see you around."

When he was gone, the crew chief said, "I'm impressed. You apparently have friends in high places."

"What's that supposed to mean?"

"Well, I don't quite know how to say it," the crew chief said, suddenly embarrassed.

53

"Let's have it, sergeant," Bill said.

"Well, no disrespect meant, Mr. Byrnes. But you're the first warrant officer I've ever seen Gowald be nice to."

"Is that so?"

"He says in the old Army you had to have ten, fifteen years' service before you could think of getting to be a warrant."

"He's right," Bill said.

"Well, I'll tell you this, him liking you won't do you no harm around here," the crew chief said. "He's what they call one of the power elite."

"If he's anything like Finnegan," Bill said. "He knows just about as much about what's going on as the battalion commander."

"Who knows as much as the battalion commander?" It was Halverson. Bill hadn't seen him come up.

"I was suggesting, sir, that a senior noncom, a good one, often knows as much as the commanding officer about . . ."

"I don't think that's true," Halverson said. "Otherwise he'd *be* an officer."

Bill bit off the reply that came to him.

"I think we'd better get this machine preflighted, don't you?" Halverson said.

"I've preflighted it, sir," Bill said.

"I'll check it, too," Halverson said. This wasn't Flight School any more, Bill thought, suddenly angry, where everything was double-checked as part of training. He had just been insulted.

"Yes, sir," Bill said.

They had completed the preflight and strapped themselves in their seats, and Bill had gotten as far on the check-list as "Starter Ignition Switch" before he realized suddenly that this flight, no matter what similarities there were to the ones before, was like no other he'd ever been on before. This was no training flight; this was an operational flight.

He wasn't scared, and he wondered why. Everybody was supposed to be scared. He had been around the Army too long to believe in icy calm heroes.

But the fact was, he wasn't afraid.

"This is Lily Baker One," Halverson's voice said in his earphones. "Report in."

"Lily Baker Two, cranked," a voice said, and then others. "Baker Three, cranked." "Baker Four, cranked." The five other aircraft commanders in the other ships of the flight were reporting that they had started their engines and were prepared to proceed with the mission.

"Tiger-Lily, Lily Baker One," Halverson said.

"Go ahead, Baker One," the tower replied.

"Tiger-Lily Baker, a flight of six, prepared to take off separately," Halverson said.

"Tiger-Lily Baker is cleared for running takeoff on a heading of zero seven five," the tower replied. "The time is one hundred twenty, the winds are negligible and the altimeter is three zero zero zero."

"Lily Baker One to Lily Baker," Halverson said. "We will take off on a heading of zero seven five, climbing to five five hundred, forming on me in two V's. Baker One out." He turned to Bill and pointed to the controls. "Yours, Mr. Byrnes," he said.

Bill put his hands to the controls.

"Permission to take off, sir?"

"Let's go, Mr. Byrnes," Halverson said.

Bill pulled up on the collective. When the Huey grew light on the skids, he lowered the nose. When he was airborne, he turned the aircraft with the anti-torque pedals under his feet until the compass before him showed a heading of 075 degrees. Then he lowered the nose a little more and the Huey moved across the ground, ever faster. He pulled up on the collective and it soared into the air. The altimeter began to wind up. On either side he could see the noses of the other two helicopters in his V, assuming their formation flight positions as they climbed to the prescribed altitude. Halverson sat beside him, his arms folded on his chest.

When they reached 5,500 feet, Bill leveled off.

"We're at altitude and on heading, sir," he said.

"Presuming we didn't leave our gunner and the crew chief on the ground, Mr. Byrnes," Halverson said, "I suppose everything is hunky-dory."

"Sorry, sir," Bill said. He was ashamed. He had forgotten to check, to ask the crew chief and the gunner if they were ready to take off.

"Don't forget again, Mr. Byrnes," Halverson said. He reached into the calf pocket of his flight suit and took out a celluloid-covered low-level chart of this area of Vietnam. He found their destination and marked it with a grease pencil. Then he wrote the call sign of the infantry unit and the FM frequency they would use beside it.

"I'll work the radio, Mr. Byrnes," he said. "You pay attention."

"Yes, sir."

There was a faint clicking noise in Bill's earphones as

the frequency of the ground troops was tuned in, and then Halverson's voice:

"Comanche Victor Six, this is Tiger-Lily Baker, over."

The reply was clear but faint.

"This is Comanche Victor, go ahead Tiger-Lily Baker."

"We are about ten minutes out," Halverson said. "Are you ready for us?"

"Standing by, Tiger-Lily. Comanche Victor out."

Halverson next said to Bill:

"They'll blow some purple smoke when they have us in sight. Land the section so that the smoke grenade is just to the right rear of Number Two."

Bill nodded his understanding, then said, "Yes, sir." He understood what he was expected to do. The six Hueys of the section called Tiger-Lily Baker were flying in two V elements, each composed of three aircraft. The lead ship, his, was Number One. Number Two was the distance of two rotor discs to his right rear. Number Three was to the left of, and parallel with, Number Two. Number Four led the second section, two rotor discs' distance behind the first three ships, with numbers Five and Six to his right and left rear.

When he landed to pick up their infantry passengers, Halverson wanted him to land so that the smoke grenade identifier would be to the right of the middle part of the flight.

"Overfly the destination," Halverson said, "and come down fast in a circle to the left."

"Yes, sir," Bill said.

He understood this, too. He had been taught at Fort Rucker that the Viet Cong would often sneak machine guns in near a place where helicopters might land. A gradual descent made too good a target. A steep descent, almost a dive for a helicopter, made it harder for the Viet Cong gunners.

But from where he sat, with Vietnam spread out peacefully beneath him like a soft green blanket, it was difficult to believe that people down there would make a serious effort to kill him.

The radio spoke again, more distinctly this time.

"Tiger-Lily Baker," the voice said. "I think I have you in sight. Blowing smoke."

Bill instinctively looked out and down but could see nothing.

"Hard to see from up here," Halverson said, as if reading his mind. "I give you twenty seconds to overfly. Mark time. Mark."

Bill looked at the sweep second hand of the clock on the instrument panel. Twenty seconds after Lieutenant Halverson said, "Mark," he gently lowered his collective pitch lever and pushed the cyclic control very slightly forward and to the left. From the corners of his eyes, he saw the two Hueys beside him duplicate his movement. Almost immediately, he could feel, from the pressure in his ears, the effect of the rapid change of altitude. The needle on the airspeed indicator rose to the red-line mark at 120 knots. He compensated for this by decreasing the speed of his descent.

The tachometer showed that the engine was in the green at 6500 rpm and the rotor in the green at about 310 rpm. As the turn neared completion, he could see the landing zone out his left window, and now he saw the plume of purple smoke rising almost straight up in the air. He didn't have to look at the altimeter any more. He was low enough to judge his distance from the ground by eye.

"Tiger-Lily Baker on final," Halverson said over the radio.

Bill pulled, ever so gently, on the cyclic control between his legs. This made the nose of the helicopter rise, and turned the air mass into a sort of brake. The airspeed kept dropping as they neared the ground. About five feet off the ground, he pulled up on the collective. The helicopter hovered motionless over the ground.

Then he decreased his pressure on the collective and the helicopter settled. He felt the skids touch, and then he was on the ground. He moved the throttle to ground idle and looked at Lieutenant Halverson.

Almost immediately, he felt the Huey buck and lurch as the infantrymen jumped aboard. He turned and watched as they boarded the machine with a skill that could only be born of practice.

He found himself looking into the face of a young soldier. The face was almost hidden behind camouflage grease paints, shades of brown and green and black, and under a helmet whose net covering had been stuck full of branches and leaves. The soldier looked back at him, and Bill saw that he was frightened.

And when he saw that, Bill became frightened himself.

"All aboard, sir," the crew chief's voice came over the intercom.

"Very good," Halverson said. "Tiger-Lily Baker, report."

"Two, ready," the radio replied immediately, and then there was a pause.

"Three?" Halverson demanded, impatiently.

"Three ready, sir," the radio said, and then "Four" "Five" and "Six" reported in.

"I've got it, Mr. Byrnes," Halverson said, and Bill took his hands off the control and his feet off the pedals. He held his hands open and in front of him to show that he had understood and complied with Halverson's order to turn command of the helicopter over to him.

"Baker One," Halverson said. "Here we go."

Bill watched the control panel as the tachometer showed the engine rpm and then the rotor rpm increase to speeds which would permit takeoff. The Huey was heavy now, with ten fully-equipped troops riding in the back. A running takeoff was necessary with this much weight. The Huey seemed reluctant to fly, and then reluctant to gain speed, but Halverson got it into the air, and began a slow climbing turn to the right. In this attitude, the Huey was most vulnerable, because it couldn't maneuver well. Right now it didn't matter. But should it be necessary to make what the Army called a "tactical extraction," or "tac-extract," of troops from the assault area, it would be very dangerous, for then they could expect Viet Cong gunners to be on the high points.

"This is Gilded Lily," the radio said. Bill recognized Major Kramer's voice. "Report."

"Able on heading three minutes out from control point at altitude," a voice said.

"Baker on heading, passing four thousand, five minutes from control point," Halverson reported.

"Guns at control point, sir," a third voice said, and Bill recognized it as Captain Hawker's.

"Dog on Baker's tail, sir," another voice said.

60

Ahead of him, Bill could see the Huey gunships, thirty or forty of them in V's of five helicopters each, traveling in a wide circle. Approaching them was Able Section, six helicopters. Apparently another six choppers, Dog Section, were behind Bill's flight.

"All elements," a new voice said. "We are commencing artillery."

There was something about the tone of voice that told Bill this was the combat assault's senior commander, even before he reached this conclusion logically by deciding that only the commander would make an announcement like this.

Somewhere down below, lanyards were being pulled and 155-mm. and 175-mm. rifles were firing projectiles weighing hundreds of pounds at the assault area. They would fire steadily, as rapidly as they could be reloaded, for as long as the barrage lasted.

He had to devote his attention to what was happening now as the various elements of Tiger-Lily joined up. Ten of the gunships took the lead in the ever-widening circle, flying in two V's of five Hueys. As Able's six helicopters joined, V's of three-chopper gunships took up positions on either side of them.

And then three Huey V's took up position on either side of Tiger-Lily Baker as they joined the circle.

"Baker in position, the gunships have joined," Halverson reported.

"Roger, Baker," Kramer's voice came over the radio.

"Have no fear, Baron von Beethoven is here," another voice, obviously disguised, called over the radio.

"That'll be enough of that," Kramer's voice said, sharply.

"*Jawohl,* Herr General," the voice said, undaunted.

"Dog in position, the guns are with us," the Dog Section flight leader reported.

"Lily ready to go, sir," Kramer's voice said.

"Roger, Lily," the authoritative voice which had announced the beginning of the artillery barrage replied.

There was no sound for more than two minutes as the mass of helicopters, a strange fleet of odd-shaped aircraft, moved in a wide orbit over the thick vegetation below. Then the commander's voice came over the air again.

"Farragut Leader, this is Galahad Six. I have sixty seconds to Time Mike."

"Roger, Galahad Six, this is Farragut Leader. We will commence run in sixty seconds from hack." There was a pause, then "Hack."

Bill watched as the sweep-second hand on the instrument panel clock moved around.

In forty-five seconds from "Hack," still another new voice said, "Barrage lifted in zero five seconds. Four three two one. Lifted."

"Farragut Leader to Galahad Six, we are commencing run."

It was the first time Bill had even seen the jets. They came in, nine of them, three V's of Navy F11F jets, dropping out of the sky to pass beneath the circle of helicopters, moving fast and barely visible against the ground. They bored in toward the thin column of smoke marking the assault area, firing rockets and machine guns and dropping napalm. Smoke began to rise from the jungle. Then there came a sort of dull glow under the canopy of forest, which erupted into flaming debris.

"Secondary explosion," Halverson said over the intercom. "Looks like we hit an ammo dump. Charlie's in there all right."

And then there was Major Kramer's voice.

"This is Gilded Lily," he said. "Commence assault."

The gunships in the lead of the circling helicopters began a steep descent to the right. Bill Byrnes, Warrant Officer Junior Grade, nineteen years old, co-pilot of Tiger-Lily Baker One, looked at his hands. They were shaking, and they were covered with cold sweat. He was afraid, after all.

## ❀ 5 ❀

THERE WAS no question about which of the cleared areas below and ahead of them was to be the landing zone. No map was needed. The landing zone erupted in flame and smoke as rockets and machine-gun bullets tore into it and beyond it into the thick forest.

The first wave of armed Hueys, the guns, flashed across the landing zone, firing machine guns and rockets, and then turned — broke — to the right and to the left. The second wave of Hueys came onto the target just as the first wave left, so there was never a moment that the target wasn't under attack. The fire was directed into the forest now, and as the second wave turned to the left and right, the third wave of guns came in. By this time the first wave had completed its circle and was back.

Then the personnel and cargo haulers, the slicks of Tiger-Lily, were approaching the landing zone, flying in two V's. As they neared the LZ, their crew chiefs and gunners began to fire the door machine guns.

The noses rose, and the Hueys flared out, hovering two or three feet off the ground. From either side, the infantrymen jumped out. Some sought the first cover they came across. Others ran to the trees. No sooner was the last infantryman out than the choppers began to rise again into the sky, their door machine guns firing steadily at the trees.

It was Baker's turn now.

"Here we go," Halverson said. He steered the helicopter down to the ground, flared it out and hovered. The troops started to jump out. The helicopter felt noticeably lighter.

There was a sudden sound. "Thu-wack."

"Uh-oh," Halverson said. He made a face as if he had sucked on a lemon.

Then the noise came again. "Thu-wack. Thu-wack."

"There he is," Halverson said. "Can't you see him?"

The Baker One machine gun behind Bill's ear let out a long burst, the noise muffled, fortunately, by his crash helmet and thick rubber radio earphones. Every fifth bullet was a tracer, and Bill watched as the whizzing flashes moved across the treeline and then paused at what looked at first like a fallen tree. Then he saw the barrel behind the tree, and the sandbags supporting it. The flashes from the Huey's door machine gun now pointed right at the barrel. A couple of ricocheted tracers sailed skyward and then the barrel of the Viet Cong gun itself pointed toward the sky, obviously no longer guided. The helicopter machine gun stopped firing.

"What have we got?" Halverson asked.

Bill ran his eyes over the instruments on the control panel. "All green, sir," he said.

"How's it back there? We got any visible leaks?"

"Looks OK, sir," the crew chief said, and in a moment the gunner said the same thing.

"Here we go," Halverson said. He pulled the helicopter off the ground rapidly and banked steeply to the right, making a running takeoff at full military power, and clearing the trees by five feet.

As they turned they could see Dog Section coming in on its final approach with the gunships protecting it, firing their machine guns and rockets into the treeline.

"Take over, Mr. Byrnes," Halverson said, and Bill put his hands and feet on the controls. Halverson unstrapped himself from his seat and stepped between the seats into the rear of the helicopter. Bill knew that he was looking for damage from the bullets that had hit the ship, but he couldn't take his eyes from his flying to watch. He was aware, however, that Number Two and Number Three ships had resumed their positions to his right and left.

Halverson came forward again, strapped himself back in, and there was the click as he reconnected his intercom system.

"Right through us," he said. "No major damage." Then, without waiting for a reply, he said, "Report."

One by one, the other five helicopter commanders reported their status. Four wholly untouched. Number Five, however, had a wounded gunner.

"How bad is he?" Halverson asked.

"He took a bullet, probably from a submachine gun, in his leg," the reply came.

"You come with us," Halverson ordered. "We'll get you a replacement gunner, and you can be the first ship to go on dustoff. That'll get him to the hospital fastest."

"Roger, sir, thank you," the aircraft commander reported.

Ahead and below on the ground, Bill could see the resupply point. What looked like blunt-ended footballs were actually fuel cells, huge rubber tanks which had been carried to the supply point slung beneath twin-engined, twin-rotored Chinook helicopters. Elsewhere on the open area were ammunition resupply points and, waiting for the helicopters, the second wave of infantrymen, broken down into the small groups which each helicopter could carry.

The element of surprise was now gone. Resupply from now on would be directly from this point to the landing zone, rather than via the orbit point where they had formed for the first assault.

Halverson took over the controls again as they came close to the ground, and Bill had the opportunity to look around. He saw Number Five leave the formation and flutter down beside a Red Cross flag pegged flat on the ground. Before the helicopter actually touched the ground, three men ran out to it from a tent which had red crosses painted on its roof.

Despite all the firing, and all the activity, Bill had seen only three actual signs of war. He had seen an enemy machine gun (but not the gunners) and he had heard the thuwack of bullets hitting the helicopter (but he had not seen any holes, and the noise wasn't the noise he had expected from the movies). And then there was the wounded man on Number Five. He thought of this, and looked down at his hands. They weren't sweaty and they were no longer shaking. He'd been too busy, he decided, to stay scared.

The second wave of troops jumped aboard, and in less than forty-five seconds they were airborne again. Number Five stayed on the ground, waiting for the first call for a Medical Evacuation helicopter — a Dustoff.

The second landing was uneventful. If they were fired on, they weren't hit. There was no way to tell if you were being fired on unless you were hit, or unless by a freak

67

of circumstance you happened to see the flash of the enemy gun. The noise of the helicopter engine and the rotors and the radio in your ears made it impossible to pinpoint sound.

By the time they landed for the second time, the fire of the gunships still circling overhead had been directed farther into the forest, as the troops penetrated deeper. There was organization now on the landing zone. There were stacks of ammunition and supplies. Guides waited for the second wave troops, to show them where to go. A medical team had a Red Cross flag flying and as Halverson lost forward speed and prepared to settle to the ground, Bill saw a stretcher-bearer crew trot across the field toward the flag. For a moment he was confused. The man on the stretcher, already wearing a bandage on his chest, seemed to have lost almost all of his uniform. He had neither shirt nor fatigue trousers nor jungle boots. Then Bill got a closer look. He wasn't a GI. He was obviously the enemy, captured, and now getting the same medical treatment given the men whom ten minutes before he had been trying to kill.

"Take it out of here, Mr. Byrnes," Halverson said, jerking Bill rudely from his spectator's role. Bill put his hands on the controls, ran his eyes down the control panel, and took off.

The rest of the afternoon passed very quickly, more quickly than Bill could ever remember time having passed before. He lost count of the number of flights he made from the supply point to the landing zone. He had no idea which times he had flown and which times he had simply sat there with his feet tucked under his seat, his arms folded over his chest.

All of a sudden he became aware that darkness was coming on, that the sharp details of the terrain beneath him were very rapidly fading. Then the radio had a message for them.

"Tiger-Lily Baker, this is Gilded Lily."

"Go ahead, Gilded Lily."

"Baker One, can you make it into the LZ once more without flares?"

"Affirmative."

"There's an eight-man pickup to be made. Will you make it?"

"Roger."

"Have the rest of the flight report to base."

"Roger, Lily Baker out. Lily Baker Two, take over the flight and return to base."

"Roger, Baker One."

They had been flying empty, headed toward the supply point. Now Halverson dipped the nose of the Huey and made a turn to the left. The rest of the flight kept its position until Number Two had moved into the lead spot and then, together, they banked to the right and headed home. There was one more radio transmission. In a thick, mock-German accent, a voice said:

"As duh sun sink slowly in duh vest, ve bid farevell to Baron von Beethoven and his Flying Circus."

"I know who that was," Halverson said, suddenly, angrily. "I'll see you on the ground, Wilson."

"Who, me, sir?" a voice said.

"The phantom strikes again," the voice — obviously not Wilson's — said. *"Auf Wiedersehen,* Herr Baron."

Bill looked at Halverson. The way the sun was striking

the sun visor of his helmet, Bill could see through it, and saw that Halverson was smiling. It was the first time he had ever seen him smile.

"I'd have sworn that was Wilson," he said, and actually laughed over the intercom. Then he got down to business. "Comanche Victor Six, this is Tiger-Lily Baker, to make a personnel pickup, about five minutes out from the LZ."

"Lily Baker, report on short final and we'll fire yellow smoke."

"Roger, understand yellow."

It wouldn't be yellow smoke, of course. The enemy was listening to the radio conversation and that would simply be making a target of yourself. With the signal operating instructions had been the color code for that operation. A call for yellow smoke would, for example, result in green smoke. Or a call for green, in red. It was a simple code, but effective.

As they dropped lower and closer to the LZ, Bill could see that the activity had slowed down. He saw, too, that the assault had cost at least one totally wrecked Huey. It lay on its side, its rotor blades bent at right angles halfway down their length, the fuselage shattered just aft of the cabin. And as they came even closer, he saw a Chinook stagger into the air with another Huey slung beneath it, swaying gently. It didn't appear to have any structural damage at all. It could have been a simple mechanical failure, the sort of thing that happens at some time to all flying machines. Or, more likely, an enemy bullet had shattered a fuel line or an oil line and the pilot had had to shut it down and leave it there for the aerial rescue service.

"Lily Baker on final," Halverson said.

"Have you in sight, Baker," the ground commander replied. In a moment, Bill actually saw the soldier pull the pin on a smoke grenade, and in a moment, green smoke began to billow.

Halverson landed within two feet of the smoke grenade. First an officer came toward them, and then, prodded by M–16 rifles in the hands of two military policemen, four bound and blindfolded Viet Cong.

The crew chief jumped to the ground and he and the officer hauled the prisoners into the helicopter. One of the MP's got aboard and rested his back against the pilot's seat. The other MP and the officer went back out of sight, to return in a moment with another prisoner. This one was talking, in French-accented but fluent English.

"I am an officer and demand the full protection of the Geneva Convention," he said, "I demand to know where I am being taken."

"Where was the Geneva Convention when you shot the medics?" the MP said.

"That's enough of that," the American officer said. Then, to the Viet Cong officer: "You're being taken to an officer interrogation point by military aircraft, captain. Please get on the helicopter."

"I demand the full protection of the Geneva Convention," the Viet Cong captain repeated.

"You heard the lieutenant, captain," the MP said. "Now get on the chopper or I'll put you on."

The prisoner climbed aboard somewhat awkwardly, because his hands were bound. He was put in a seat, and the seat belt fastened around his waist, and then he was blindfolded.

"Any time you're ready," the officer said.

"Take us home, Mr. Byrnes, please," Lieutenant Halverson said, and held his hands in front of him to show he had relinquished command of the helicopter. Bill opened the throttle, and when the engine and rotor rpm indicators moved into the green he hauled up on the collective. It was getting dark. In another ten minutes, they wouldn't have been able to make it without lights.

By the time they got back to Pleiku it was really dark and they had to call for lights. When they landed, a three-quarter-ton truck with MILITARY POLICE painted on it was waiting for them. The prisoners were loaded aboard, and then Halverson indicated to Bill with a gesture of his hands that he should move the helicopter across the field to their tie-down position.

The rest of the flight was waiting for them, sprawled all over two helicopters. When Halverson appeared, they got to their feet.

"We've got a crank time of dawn," he said. "I want these things fueled tonight. You can either arm now or early in the morning. If you arm now, I want one man here all night for each two helicopters. Arrange it any way you want to between yourselves. But I mean here and awake. Now what about aircraft condition?"

One by one the crew chiefs reported mechanical, electrical or electronic difficulty with their helicopters. Halverson listened and gave specific instructions in each case. He might be a little starchy, Bill thought, but there was no question that he was a good officer. Then he remembered that Halverson had been smiling about the Baron von Beethoven business. That meant he had a sense of humor and wasn't entirely a martinet.

He had just come to this warming conclusion when Halverson turned on him.

"Co-pilots make out the Dash-One," he said. "And you are no exception, Mr. Byrnes. When you've completed the Dash-One, and after you've seen to the correction of any Red X's, report to me in my tent, and I'll sign off the flight plan."

"Yes, sir."

"In the case of this aircraft, we will arm tonight."

"Yes, sir."

"That's all, gentlemen," Halverson said. "Good night."

When he was out of earshot, one of the other warrant officer pilots said, "Somebody ought to tell him that no matter how hard he tries, they're not going to make him Chief of Staff until he's dry behind the ears."

There was laughter at this, and then they broke up, to repair and refuel and rearm their helicopters.

Bill found the three bullet holes in the helicopter. Actually, there were five holes. Three entry holes, rather small, and two exit holes, somewhat larger. The third bullet had apparently gone out the open door. He felt a small chill when he realized that when it had gone out the door it had passed within a foot or so of his head.

Patching the holes wouldn't be difficult. They had missed the structural frame of the fuselage. Actually, they could be patched effectively with a square inch of masking tape. But Halverson wouldn't stand for that. They would have to be covered with a small square of duraluminum, riveted in place.

The crew chief said he could handle that. Bill took the gunner and went with him to the ammunition dump. Sergeant Gowald was still on duty, sitting almost regally behind a desk, and trying to give the impression he wasn't minutely examining everything that was going on in the corrugated steel shed. When he saw Bill, however, he got to his feet and called, "Attention."

From the confusion on the faces of the others in the shed, Bill could tell they weren't used to being braced by the appearance of a lowly warrant officer. Gowald saluted and said, parade ground formal, "Good evening, sir."

Bill, somewhat embarrassed, returned the salute and called, "Rest!" to the others.

"How can we help you, sir?" Gowald asked.

"We're going to rearm tonight, Sergeant," Bill said. "We came to draw our load."

"Yes, sir," Gowald said. He looked quickly about the room, laid his eye on a tall, skinny specialist fifth class, and said, "Meredith, you heard the officer. Or do you expect him to haul his own ammo like he was some fuzzy-cheeked PFC?"

The spec five was surprised, almost shocked, and Bill immediately understood that normally warrant officers, fuzzy-cheeked or not, did indeed haul their own ammo around here.

"I'll get it, Sergeant," the spec five said, but there was questioning written all over his face.

"Why don't you come back with me in the ordnance office, Mr. Byrnes? You look like you could stand a cup of coffee."

"Thank you," Bill said. He didn't really want any coffee, but there didn't seem to be much he could do about it.

He followed Gowald out of the open room into a partitioned-off office. On a rough table sat a restaurant-type two-burner coffee brewer. Master Sergeant Gowald took two china mugs, decorated with the likenesses of young ladies not wearing very many clothes, filled them from one of the stainless-steel pots, and then handed one to Bill.

"Bottoms up," he said, and winked. Bill took a small sip and almost spit it out. It wasn't coffee.

"Twelve-year-old Kentucky sour mash bourbon," Master Sergeant Gowald explained with some pride. "Scrounged it from the general's orderly." Then his face fell. "Maybe you don't drink yet?"

"It's not that, Sergeant," Bill said. "It's just that I've got to report to Lieutenant Halverson when I'm finished. And . . ."

"And he's kind of GI, ain't he?" Gowald said, taking the mug back, carefully pouring the bourbon back into the stainless-steel coffee pot and then filling it again from the second pot. "We keep coffee in this one," he said.

"Thanks," Bill said.

"You'll notice I said GI and not chicken. There's a difference. If I have to tell you that."

"He strikes me as being a pretty good officer," Bill said.

"He gets a little older," Sergeant Gowald said, "he'll learn how to get along a little better. Me, I learned a long time ago that you have to be careful of officers who try to be good guys. They get you killed."

"I suppose that's so," Bill said.

"Now your daddy, boy, he's always been starchy."

I might as well have it out now, Bill decided.

"I don't know how to say this, Sergeant," he said. "But I'd just as soon you forgot who my father is."

"I couldn't do that, really," Gowald said. "I been knowing your daddy a long time. We walked back down from the Yalu together. I couldn't forget that. But I could forget that you're related, if that's what you're asking."

"Please."

"Irish told me you had a falling out. He didn't tell me why."

"I quit the Point," Bill said.

"You're out of your cotton-picking mind, that's what you are. No wonder he's sore."

Bill didn't reply. He couldn't get angry at this old-time noncom, but neither did he appreciate the lecture.

"Then how come you're here?" Gowald asked.

"I got drafted."

"Boy, that's something. Somebody with your blood letting himself get drafted." Bill opened his mouth to reply, but Gowald, sensing he had gone a little too far, instantly changed the subject. "How'd it go today?"

"All right. I wasn't as afraid as I thought I would be."

"You never are, when you get right down to it," Gowald said. "Take any hits?"

"Three. From a machine gun. The door gunner got him."

There was a knock at the door.

"I've got Mr. Byrnes's ammo loaded on a jeep, Sergeant," the spec five said. "Want me to take it down to the flight line for him?"

"I'll take it down," Gowald said. "I'm headed home, anyway." He stood up and looked at Bill. "If you're ready, sir?"

"Thank you, Sergeant," Bill said. They both understood the thanks were for far more than having the basic load of ammunition put aboard a jeep.

76

# ❋ 6 ❋

LIEUTENANT HALVERSON was alone in his tent, just climbing into a freshly laundered khaki uniform, when Bill came in and reported to him.

"Red X's taken care of, fuselage repaired, and the aircraft is fueled and armed, sir. The crew chief made a deal with Number Six. They'll each take two hours guarding it overnight." He handed the flight plan to Halverson.

"Very good, Mr. Byrnes," he said. "You apparently have the makings of a good officer."

There was only one thing Bill could say in reply to that, and he said it:

"Thank you, sir."

"How about a beer, Mr. Byrnes? And then a steak? I'm hungry and thirsty."

"Thank you, sir," Bill said.

"I'll drop the flight plan by Base Ops and get tomorrow's signal operating plan," Halverson said. "I'll meet you at the club. That'll give you time to shower."

"Thank you, sir," Bill said. Halverson opened the door to his wall locker to get his hat. Almost shyly, he said, pointing to a formal portrait of an attractive young woman with a little boy on her lap. "My family, Mr. Byrnes."

"Very attractive, sir."

"There'll be another one in a week or so," Halverson said. "I wish I was home for that."

Bill had a nasty thought, but he didn't say it. He thought: Don't expect me to feel sorry for you, friend. I've been through this. If you want to be home when your kids are born, get out of the Army.

After he'd thought it, he was only mildly ashamed of himself. It might not be kind, but it was true.

Halverson was waiting at the crude bar of the officers' club when Bill got there, still a little damp from a quick shower. Through the window of the small building Bill could see a charcoal stove, made from a cut- down 55-gallon drum, smouldering in the slight breeze. When they'd had a can of beer, they went outside and fed themselves. One insulated food container contained raw steaks. As these broiled on the charcoal, they took vegetables and bread and baked potatoes from other food containers.

They ate at a small table, and when they were just about through, the lights inside the club went out and a 16-mm projector began showing a movie. This was the way to go to war, Bill decided, thinking of the infantrymen who were still out there in the DZ, fighting insects and snakes and Viet Cong. In these circumstances, a man who had a shower and a change of clothes and a steak and a beer was a rich man. At half past ten, when he slid between the crisp sheets on his bed, he lay awake a long time, thinking. He had gone to war. Today, a stranger had tried to kill him and almost succeeded. He had gone to war, and then he had come home and had a beer and a steak and gone to bed.

At dawn, having eaten, and gone through both tactical and weather briefings, he was in the co-pilot's seat again, waving his finger in a circular motion to the crew chief, and announcing through his mike that they were about to crank.

They flew resupply missions to the same drop zone all day, stopping only for an incongruous lunch complete with salad and ice cream, served in the shade of a fly tent at the resupply point. When he turned the flight plan over to Lieutenant Halverson that night, he saw that they had spent almost nine hours in the air. That was a lot of flying, and he was tired.

The second night was very much like the first. He had his meal and a beer in the officers' club, exchanging small talk with Halverson, neither of them offering much personal information about themselves, never once letting military courtesy lapse between them.

And the third day and the third night were very much like the second. Bill liked to fly with Halverson. Halverson was a skilled pilot, but more than that he was a natural pilot. Even his most violent maneuvers seemed well coordinated. And they developed an unspoken understanding, meshing their skills so that there was seldom a hesitation, seldom a duplication of effort. They became a team.

Bill learned, too, the names (instead of just the ranks and last names) of the crew chief and the gunner. On the fourth day, he asked and received permission to take a Bell H−13, the now nearly obsolete two-seater that had served so well in Korea, and flew Eddie, the gunner, from Pleiku over the Mang Yang Pass to the hospital at An Khe, so that he could carry mail and a package to the gunner who had been wounded on Bill's first combat assault.

They had to stay up most of the night when they got back, getting the Huey in shape for the next day's operation, but it seemed worth the effort. If Bill had been in the hospital, he would have appreciated having someone haul him his mail and a package from home.

By the time he had been in Vietnam a month, he had decided that the element of risk in helicopter operations had been exaggerated. It might be a tough war, it *was* a tough war, for the poor guys in the infantry, but the chopper jockeys had it pretty good.

On the anniversary of his first month in Vietnam, Warrant Officer Junior Grade Wilson Campbell Byrnes participated as co-pilot in his eleventh combat assault. They took a few hits in the side of the fuselage, but no one was wounded, and the helicopter was patched and fueled and armed within two hours of their landing at Pleiku. An hour after that, Warrant Officer Byrnes was Officer In Charge of Brushing the Barbecue Sauce on a rather tasty-looking rack of spareribs on the charcoal outside the club, when Major Kramer appeared and attracted attention by thumping on the round sides of the grill with a beer bottle.

"I need four crews to make a tactical evacuation," he said. "Charlie's hit a Special Forces camp and they're apparently in bad shape."

When Lieutenant Halverson stood up, Bill automatically walked to his side.

"That's one crew," Kramer said. "Hawke and I will go. We need six more pilots."

One by one, six pilots stepped forward.

A tactical evacuation was a military euphemism for sticking your neck out. It meant a mission so dangerous it would not otherwise be flown, if the tactical situation didn't absolutely require it. When the term tactical evacuation was used, it meant Charlie had successfully applied the philosophy of Mao Tse Tung and Ho Chi Minh. He had attacked with forces so superior nothing could stop him. And the defenders, who could not retreat or withdraw down a highway, had to be evacuated by air, by helicopter.

It was a risky operation for a number of reasons. For one thing, since it was necessary to make the evacuation in the first place, it was almost a sure thing that Charlie would have machine guns trained on the landing zone. Secondly, since they would be landing empty and taking off full, they would lurch and stagger into the air. It would be just the reverse of landing full and taking off empty and highly maneuverable.

"We'll crank as soon I brief the pilots," Kramer said. "Co-pilots, get on with the preflight."

"What about lights, Major?"

"We've got Air Force flares on the way," Kramer said. "And so's Puff the Magic Dragon from the First Air Command Wing. The people upstairs want a quick extraction, so they can bomb the place. I guess they've even got the B–52's on the way."

Puff the Magic Dragon was the very nice name for a very nasty and very unusual weapon of war. It was actually made up of two obsolete items. The old Gatling gun of the Spanish-American War, had been upped in power to 7.62 mm, and was now turned by an electric motor instead of a crank, so that it could fire 6,000 rounds per minute. Three of these weapons were mounted in an Air Force C–47, which had actually been declared obsolete before World War II, despite the service it had rendered there as the standard transport.

There was no joke about it being a dragon, however. Bill had seen it demonstrated by the Air Force Air Commandos at Hurlburt Field, just across the Florida border near Fort

Rucker. When the pilot let loose he was firing 18,000 rounds per minute. It did indeed breathe fire.

"How come just four Hueys?" a voice called.

"Four from us, four from the One Ninety-third. The reserves. The CA for tomorrow is still on."

In a pinch, Bill thought, they could get twelve, maybe fourteen people on a Huey, especially the much lighter Vietnamese. Twelve people times eight helicopters is ninety-six. The normal strength of a Special Forces camp was about that of a company, with an American Special Forces team of anywhere from eight to thirty, and the rest Vietnamese troops. That meant they'd have to make two evacuations each. Presuming nobody got shot down. If they lost helicopters, that would mean three evacuations under fire.

Those were not very attractive odds.

There was no shortage of enlisted volunteers. Three quarters of the crew chiefs and gunners were gathered around Base Operations. A full head over most of them, stood Master Sergeant Gowald.

"You're a little old for this sort of thing, aren't you, Sergeant?" Major Kramer asked.

"You add up me and Mr. Byrnes, Major," Gowald replied with the assurance of the old soldier, "and divide by two, and it'll come out all right."

There was delighted laughter at this.

"You ride gunner with me, Gowald," Kramer said.

"Yes, sir," Gowald said.

By the time Lieutenant Halverson climbed in the helicopter and strapped himself in place, the engine was running and warm and the rotor turning. He handed Bill his clipboard and Bill took the flashlight with the red shield over the lens and read the frequencies and call signs.

"Let's hear it when you're ready," Kramer's voice came over the radio.

"Is that Dogcatcher Six?" a voice asked.

"Roger."

"This is Catchaser Six," the voice said. "I guess you've got date of rank, don't you, Dutch?"

"I guess I do," Kramer said, confirming that he was the senior officer present.

"OK, Dutch," the voice said. "Catchaser Six plus three more ready to go on your signal."

"Hold one, Catchaser," Kramer's voice said. "Dogcatcher, report in."

The clipboard before him identified his helicopter as Dogcatcher Two. Bill pulled his microphone trigger switch all the way back to transmit.

"Dogcatcher Two, cranked and ready."

Two other voices followed his immediately. "Dogcatcher Three, cranked." "Four, cranked."

"Dogcatcher to all elements," Kramer's voice said. "We'll form up in the air in a two-part column — me leading the first half, Catchaser Six the second. We will go into the LZ in two columns with no more than four aircraft on the ground at any one time. No acknowledgement required. Questions?"

There was the sound of static for thirty seconds, but no voice came over the radio.

"Tiger-Lily, this is Dogcatcher Six, leading a formation of eight for takeoff."

"Tiger-Lily clears Dogcatcher flight to take off at his discretion. The time is two five past the hour. The altimeter is two niner five. The winds are from the north-northeast at one five, gusting to two five. Exercise caution."

Bill reached up and set the clock and wound it, even though it had an eight-day movement and he remembered winding it no more than two hours before. He set the barometric pressure on the altimeter, and then sat back and waited for Halverson to take them into the air.

Major Kramer's landing light went on, a bright, white beam. It moved across the runway, turned, and then made a running takeoff. Then the light went off, although they could see his red and green navigation lights.

"Landing light on," Halverson's voice said in Bill's earphones.

"On," Bill said, quite unnecessarily. It was obviously on.

"Ready in the back seat?" Halverson asked.

"Ready, sir," from the crew chief and the gunner.

"Here we go," Halverson said, and took off.

They had been up perhaps fifty seconds when a voice reported with obvious disgust:

"This is Three. I just lost oil pressure. Making an autorotation to the field."

"Four," Kramer ordered without further comment. "Move up."

"Moving up, sir."

Now there were seven helicopters.

They flew for fifteen minutes, and then Kramer's voice came over the radio.

"Romeo Six, this is Dogcatcher Six, will you give us a long count so we can get a navigational fix, please."

"Roger, Dogcatcher Six. One. Two. Three. Four. Fiver. Six. Seven. Eight. Niner. Niner. Eight. Seven. Six. Fiver. Four. Three. Two. One. Is that enough, Dogcatcher?"

"That's fine, Romeo, thank you."

As the voice had counted over the air, Bill had connected

the radio compass to the FM receiver. The needle of the compass now pointed to the radio station on the ground. Ahead of him, Major Kramer's helicopter banked slightly to the left as he pointed the machine directly toward the ground station. Almost immediately, Halverson moved their helicopter in behind him.

"Romeo, what's your situation?" Kramer's voice asked.

"Sort of hairy," the ground station replied. "I guess Charlie wants this hilltop pretty bad. Where are you guys, anyway?"

"I estimate ten minutes," Kramer said.

"Did you bring a doctor?"

"Negative. There wasn't time."

"I've got ten boys that need a doctor pretty bad."

"I'm assigning Dogcatcher Two to pick them up," Kramer said. "For direct An Khe. If you have a medic, load him aboard too."

"Thank you, Dogcatcher. We'll be standing by."

"You get that, Two?" Kramer asked.

"Roger, sir," Halverson said. Then, over the intercom, "You guys rig it up to carry wounded," he said. "And move quick when we're on the ground."

"Yes, sir."

Checking the clock, Bill had just decided that he might catch a look at where they were going by looking out over the instrument panel when he heard Kramer's voice again.

"Romeo, I see what looks like a fire ahead. Can you hear us?"

"Negative, Dogcatcher, but there's a lot of noise down here."

Even over the radio, Bill could hear small-arms fire and the peculiar "crump" of mortars.

"Are we going to be able to get in down there, Romeo?" Kramer asked.

"Well it's not O'Hare Field. We'll set up what covering fire we can, if you give us a signal when you're going to touch down. I'd stay as close to the barbed wire as I could."

"Roger, thank you," Kramer said, calmly. "I'm going to blink my landing light. Will you let me know if you see it?"

"Standing by."

Ahead, Kramer's light lit and then faded.

"I saw it. Shooting a flare," the ground commander reported. A red ball looped up from the ground.

"I have you in sight. Estimate ninety seconds to touchdown," Kramer said.

"Anytime, Dogcatcher."

"Dogcatcher to all elements. Door gunners, hold your fire unless you have a target."

"Dogcatcher, this is Puff," a new voice said.

"Go ahead, Puff."

"Dogcatcher, I'm orbiting at fifteen hundred feet and I have you in sight. When do you want me?"

"Puff, Dogcatcher. I wish you'd lay it in on our departure route. We're going to be pretty awkward at this altitude. Can I have it on signal?"

"Roger, Dogcatcher. Watch for my light."

Ahead, the twin landing lights on the Air Force C–47 flashed on and then glowed out.

"I have you in sight, Puff," Kramer said, and then, in a joking voice, "Glad to see ya."

"Catchaser?" Kramer asked.

"Anytime, Dutch."

"Romeo, let's have that covering fire," Kramer said. "Here we come."

Kramer's Huey dipped toward the ground. His landing light came on and stayed on. Halverson flew on his tail, but didn't call for the landing light until the Huey ahead obviously flared and his light went out.

"Landing light," Halverson ordered. Bill flipped the switch. He was frightened when he saw how close they had come to the ground in darkness. Almost instantly there was the thump and crunch as the skids made contact with the rocks and pierced steel planking of the helipad.

"Light out," Halverson ordered.

"Out," Bill replied. The white light had nearly blinded him, but as his pupils expanded again, he could make out the fainter orange wink of small-arms fire, and an infrequent tracer bullet making an arc in the sky. There was a bright flash in front of him, a moment's light when he could see smoke, and then he felt the concussion of a mortar round.

The Viet Cong had the landing area bracketed with mortar fire.

Another mortar went off to his right, and then another, still farther to the right. He corrected his initial judgment. The mortars were not firing accurately. Thank God for that. In the dim light of the burning equipment he saw soldiers running to Major Kramer's helicopter.

He became aware that something heavy was being loaded into his helicopter. A head appeared between the pilots' seats.

"I've got two on here that need a doc real bad," the soldier said. "We're sure glad to see you guys."

"Let's have it, Puff," Major Kramer said.

"On the way," the radio answered.

Suddenly the sky in front of them looked as if someone had turned on a monstrous neon sign. Three bands of brilliant orange fire ran from the ground up to a point in the darkness. It wasn't a sign. It was three 7.62–mm. machine guns. Puff the Magic Dragon had opened up.

Bill was fascinated by the sheer power of it. Then he became aware that Major Kramer had turned on his landing light again and that his helicopter was very slowly, obviously overloaded, trying to take off.

Bill looked over his shoulder to see how the loading of their ship was coming. As he turned, he felt the concussion of another mortar round, and then he heard a peculiar ripping tinkle.

He turned back again. There was an unusual white light coming from the instrument panel. Normally, so they could be read more easily, the instruments glowed red.

He hadn't had time to digest this when he became aware that Major Kramer's landing light, fifty feet in the air, was now pointing at the ground again. He watched in horror as Kramer's Huey hit the ground and burst into flame. He looked at Halverson.

Halverson, of all fool things, had decided to take a nap. He was leaning forward against his shoulder harness, his chin resting on his chest. Bill reached over and pushed him. There was no response. And then Bill felt something warm and sticky between the rolled-up cuff of the lieutenant's khaki shirt (there hadn't been time to put on a flight suit) and his soft leather gloves.

He knew in an instant what it was, and had an almost

irresistible urge to vomit. He managed to suppress it. The thing to do was to get out of here.

"Ready in the back?" he asked. There was no reply. The radios were apparently out. He looked over his shoulder. The cargo compartment was jammed full, and no one else seemed to be trying to get on.

The instruments on his side of the control panel were apparently working. He had oil and fuel pressure, the tail-pipe temperature was where it should be. He moved the cyclic and it turned freely, and the collective seemed to be functioning properly. But when he stepped on the foot pedals, the torque control pedal, they moved with difficulty. He leaned over and saw that Halverson's feet were still on the pedals.

He had to unstrap himself from his seat, stand up, lean over Halverson and pull his feet free of the pedals. As he did so, he made the mistake of looking at Halverson's face. Only half of it was still there.

Without bothering to strap himself in again, and deciding not to use the landing light (there was, for one thing, enough light from Kramer's burning Huey) he opened the throttle to full military emergency power and pulled up on the collective. He felt the Huey grow light on the skids and then become airborne. He lowered the nose and began to move across the strip.

Slowly, even grudgingly, the machine began to respond to his touch. He pulled higher on the collective and saw the blackness of the ground drop away beneath him.

But being airborne and alive was a long way from being safe. He soon found that he had no communications or navigation equipment at all, unless you wanted to be generous and consider the magnetic compass mounted between the windshields as a navigation instrument. If they had taken a hit bad enough to knock out Halverson's instruments, they had probably suffered other damage as well. There might be a power loss at any moment. The prospect of an autorotation into the mountainous jungle with a chopper load of badly wounded men was not pleasant.

He had only a vague idea of where he was.

He went over the alternatives available to him as he slowly gained altitude and got beyond the reach of further ground fire.

He could, assuming the compass was accurate, attempt to fly back alone. Except he didn't know the heading, so that didn't make much sense.

He could head for the South China Sea, and fly down the coast until he found a base. That was presuming he had enough fuel left, that he hadn't taken a hit in a fuel cell. If he ran out of fuel, he would go into the jungle. They wouldn't even know where to look for him.

On top of that, he had banged his knee somehow. It had really begun to hurt; he was having a hard time keeping it from shaking.

He tightened the friction lock on the collective control and took his hand from it and put it on his knee. It came away wet. He looked down and in the dull glow from the instrument panel he saw that his upper leg was blood-soaked.

He was tired and frightened and alone and he didn't know what to do, or, literally, which way to turn.

And then below him, he saw another helicopter. He remembered in that moment that one of his passengers in the rear had brought a walkie-talkie aboard. If luck was with him, maybe the Huey below was still monitoring the Fox Mike frequency used by Special Forces.

"Hey," he called, and the crew chief stuck his head between the seats.

"We lost two of these guys when that last mortar went off," the crew chief shouted. "And I guess we lost communication, too, huh?"

"Get me that PRC radio," Bill said. In a minute it was handed up to him. He slid open the window by his head and stuck the antenna out. The minute it hit the windstream, it blew flat against the door. There was no way to help that.

"Unknown Dogcatcher or Catchaser Huey, this is Dogcatcher Two. I have lost aircraft communication."

There was a long pause, and he had just about decided that this idea had failed when, very faintly against the sound of the wind, he got a reply.

"Aircraft calling Dogcatcher on Fox Mike, say again?"

"This is Dogcatcher Two at three five hundred. I have a Huey in sight. I have lost communications. Please flash landing light."

He looked out ahead. A light went on and died.

"I have you in sight. I have no radio or navigation. Please lead me home."

"Roger, Dogcatcher," the voice said. "Flash your light."

Bill flipped the switch. Nothing happened.

"I have no light," he said to the radio. This time he couldn't hear the reply.

But the other Huey seemed to slow and wait for him, and when he drew very close, a hand — probably the door gunner's — came out and waved.

It took them twenty minutes to make it back to Pleiku, and as they approached the airport lights went on.

It looks good, Bill thought. But I can't land here. I've got to go over the Pass to An Khe. If I land here, they'll never let this thing in the air again, so full of holes. It'll take them ten, fifteen minutes to transfer these guys to another chopper. When you're hurt and need a doctor, fifteen minutes is a long time.

He knew the heading of the runway. He flew over it. It differed three degrees from the heading shown on the magnetic compass. He made the mental compensation, and took up the heading that would carry him over the Mang Yang Pass to the hospital at An Khe.

The hospital was brilliantly lighted, and he had no trouble finding it or the helipads by the emergency ward. Other Hueys were on the ground, and one took off just as Bill was making his final approach. It veered sharply to the left, and Bill was sure that the pilot was saying unkind things about him.

When the Huey touched down this time, it sagged to the left. Bill wondered if it had been that bad a landing or whether the skids had been damaged by the mortar.

White-uniformed hospital corpsmen came on the run, carrying stretchers, with doctors and nurses at their side. Bill sat for a full minute before he remembered to shut down the helicopter. It seemed to take a lot of effort, and he didn't want to look to his right, where Halverson still sat slumped against his shoulder harness.

All of a sudden, his door was jerked open.

"Hey, did you know your skid's collapsed on this side?" a medic asked.

"You've got one more to take out," Bill said. "I think he's dead."

"Oh, my God," the medic said. He shouted: "Let's have a stretcher over here!"

"Are you all right?" the medic asked.

"I think so," Bill said, and then all of a sudden, without warning, he threw up. The medic pulled back and then flashed a light into the cockpit. The last thing Warrant Officer Junior Grade Byrnes heard before he passed out was the medic's matter-of-fact shout, "Make that two stretchers."

## ❀ 7 ❀

MAJOR KRAMER walked into the ward directly to Bill's bed and without any other word of greeting said, "I talked to the surgeon. You've got a minor flesh wound, and you might as well do your recuperating back at the company where we can get some work out of you."

"I thought you were dead," Bill said.

"Obviously not," Kramer said, sarcastically.

"Gowald?"

"He's down getting your personal stuff back from the admissions people," Kramer said. "You don't think much of my flying, do you, Mr. Byrnes?"

"I saw it burn. I took off with the light from your burning ship," Bill said.

"It was a little hairy for a minute or two," Kramer said, very seriously. "But we got out of it. Some of the guys in the back didn't make it."

Master Sergeant Gowald at that moment burst through the door to the ward and came marching down the center aisle.

"Good morning, sir," he boomed. "I had a hard time getting that .45 back. But here's everything, including a pair of pants with a hole in them and a fresh flight suit."

"Thanks," Bill said.

"How do you feel?" the sergeant asked, surprisingly gentle.

"I'm all right," Bill said. "The doc said I got hit with fragments of instruments, not by a mortar fragment."

"I saw the ship," Kramer said. "As a matter of fact, that's the main reason I came down here. It goes to the boneyard. What were you thinking of, flying it here after you'd made it back to Pleiku?"

"I figured if it had come that far, it would go another twenty, thirty minutes," Bill said.

"You were lucky," Kramer said. "That was a stupid thing to do."

"Luckier than Halverson," Bill said.

"Yeah," Kramer said. "I'm sorry about that." Then, abruptly, "Well, hurry up. We've been given the CA to retake that hilltop and I think you ought to go along."

"I don't suppose I could talk you into letting me stay around here and make eyes at the nurses?"

"I don't appreciate your sense of humor," Kramer said, "or, for that matter, that collegiate punk attitude of yours. I'll see you at the aircraft. Don't be long."

He walked out of the ward.

"What's with him? What's he sore about?" Bill asked.

"Halverson wasn't the only one we lost. Charlie got our Number Three and two ships from the One Ninety-third took hits. Catchaser Six bought the farm, too."

"Well, that's not my fault. What's he sore at me for?"

"He's not sore at you," Gowald said, handing him the flight suit. "He just put you in for the Distinguished Flying Cross."

"You're kidding," Bill said.

"Why? What's funny about what you did?" Gowald replied. "Can you bend that leg, or you want me to help you on with your shoe?"

"Would you, please, Sergeant?"

The leg hurt ferociously every time he moved it, or put pressure on it, but he was determined that he wouldn't let either Gowald or Major Kramer see this. On the way to Kramer's Huey, they passed the Huey Bill had flown in the night before. He didn't want to look at it, but the temptation was too great. Enlisted technicians were swarming over it. They would strip it of everything usable, and the empty fuselage would be junked.

The crew chief saw him and walked over.

"You OK, Mr. Byrnes?"

"I'm all right, thanks," Bill said. "I bent the bird pretty bad, though, didn't I?"

"You ought to see the inside of it," he said. "That thing was flying on good intentions last night." Then he paused. "Mr. Byrnes, if you're going to be looking for a crew chief, consider me a volunteer, even with all they say about not volunteering."

"They're not going to make me an aircraft commander just yet," Bill said, "but thanks for the offer."

"Any time you find it convenient, Mr. Byrnes," Major Kramer called, heavily sarcastic, "we'd like to go on with the war."

Bill walked to the ship and got in the back. A warrant was flying as co-pilot, a man he recognized only vaguely.

"I don't suppose you could have run over here, Mr. Byrnes?" Kramer pursued, sarcastically.

"No, sir, I don't think I could have run."

"See that he gets a cane, Sergeant Gowald," Kramer said.

"Yes, sir."

"Let's crank this thing up," Kramer said, and the warrant co-pilot took the checklist down. "One thing, Byrnes," Kramer said.

"Yes, sir?"

"You're the summary court officer for Lieutenant Halverson. And that includes writing a draft of a letter of sympathy to his family, for my signature. I want that done today, no matter what time we get back from the CA."

Bill started to protest, but Kramer pulled his helmet over his ears, effectively shutting off any conversation at all.

There was nothing to do now but to make himself as comfortable as possible on the flight. Very gingerly, he raised his leg, so that it rested on the olive drab nylon seat. Then he rested his back against the side of the door and watched as the crew chief stood ready with his fire extinguisher.

Kramer would just have to get someone else to write that letter of sympathy. What was he trying to do anyway? Make it worse than it was? Yesterday this time, Halverson was still sweating out the telegram from the States about his second kid. Now his wife would get a telegram. *Sorry about that, lady.*

When they landed, Bill waited patiently until Major Kramer had shut the helicopter down, until he'd spoken to the crew chief, until he looked at him.

"Something, Mr. Byrnes?"

"Sir, I've got a personal request."

"Will it hold until you get down to the orderly room and tell them you're back for duty? And until I catch the weather briefing?"

"Yes, sir," Bill said. "Of course."

Sergeant Gowald caught up with him at the orderly room.

"This is for you, sir," he said, and tossed a cane to him.

"I thought you were kidding," Bill said. "But thanks."

"Takes the weight off your leg," Gowald said. "I saw a British general one time carried one all the time, and there was nothing wrong with his leg."

"Maybe I ought to get a monocle, too," Bill said.

Bill waited until after the weather briefing before approaching Major Kramer again.

"Oh, yes, Mr. Byrnes, you and your personal problem. What is it?"

"Sir, I request to be relieved from the assignment as summary court officer for Lieutenant Halverson."

"Denied," Kramer said. "Is that all?"

"Yes, sir, that's all," Bill said.

"There are two reasons, Mr. Byrnes," Kramer said. "And, although I'm not obliged to give you either of them, I will. The first is, that of all the officers here, I think the Baron would rather have you pack his stuff to be sent home."

Bill hadn't thought of that. It was true, and it rather shamed him. It was the sort of thing Halverson would have done for him without being asked.

"I understand that you were friends, and that makes it a little hairy for you, Byrnes, but the Army just did you a favor, and turnabout seems fair play."

"The Army did me a favor?" Bill asked, and forgot for a moment to add, "Sir?"

"Your wound was initially diagnosed as serious, Mr. Byrnes. Army Regulations require that a telegram be sent to the next of kin as soon as practicable when a member of the Army suffers a serious wound, to be followed by a second telegram advising the next of kin of the prognosis and condition of the patient. I presume this isn't news to you?"

"No, sir," Bill said. It was the first time he'd thought about his mother getting the telegram.

"Sergeant Gowald checked with the hospital on your condition, and then came to me and told me that he knew your mother and suggested that it would upset the lady unnecessarily. Something to do with your tender years. Gowald should have been an insurance salesman. Anyway, when I reminded him that the regulations called for it, he suggested that I could comply with the spirit of the regulation by telephoning your next of kin, who happens to be in Vietnam. I did this, Byrnes, and there will be no telegram sent to your home."

"Oh," Bill said. Then, after a pause. "Thank you, Major. I appreciate that." That explained Gowald's presence in the hospital.

"Aren't you interested in what your father had to say?" Kramer asked.

Bill just looked at him.

"He asked if there were anything he could do; he asked that I not send the standard telegram; and he asked if I had recommended you for the Distinguished Flying Cross before or after I found out that he was a major general."

Bill still said nothing.

"You don't seem surprised about the DFC."

"Gowald told me."

"I got to An Khe about fifteen minutes after you did, with a load of wounded. I put you in for it shortly thereafter, before I had any idea who your father is."

"Yes, sir."

"I don't care who your father is, and I haven't the slightest interest in this childish fight you're having with him," Kramer said. "So long as it doesn't interfere with the efficient performance of your duty. Clear?"

"Clear, sir," Bill said.

"When we get back from this," Kramer said. "You check with the surgeon and have him inform me when you can go back on flight status."

"Yes, sir."

"And now let's get this show on the road," Kramer said. "You ride with me. That's as good a place as any."

It was a combat assault with all the trimmings: artillery and airstrikes, pass after pass by armed helicopters, and finally the landing of the slicks with their cargo of Special Forces troops bent on revenge for having been pushed off this bald patch of earth in the middle of the jungle.

But there was no resistance. The hill was deserted. Only the dead remained, and the refuse of battle.

"Charlie went back in the jungle," the Special Forces lieutenant colonel in command said. "We just shot up a lot of ordnance for nothing."

"He was here," Kramer replied. "And sometimes he stays afterward. I lost a couple of people one time when somebody decided Charlie had gone and he hadn't."

"All right," the Special Forces officer shouted, "Let's break out the body bags and get going."

The body bags were just what they sounded like: black, waterproof bags in which the bodies of the dead Americans and South Vietnamese soldiers were put so they could be loaded onto the helicopters. The Vietnamese bodies were turned over to the Vietnamese government for burial. The American bodies would be taken to Saigon where they would be embalmed and put in caskets. Each casket would be covered with an American flag, and a small ceremony would be held during which a Vietnamese officer would pin a South Vietnamese decoration to the flag. Then they'd be loaded on a jet and flown home.

Warrant Officer Junior Grade Wilson Campbell Byrnes III watched as the bags were unloaded from a helicopter. He tried not to think of Lieutenant Halverson.

What had been a combat assault now became a logistical move. A steady stream of helicopters, functioning now as aerial trucks, flew back and forth to the hilltop, bringing in fresh supplies for the reestablishment of the Special Forces camp. They brought in an awesome array of supplies.

First came the weapons of war, in case Charlie decided to attempt another attack: machine guns, mortars, ammunition, barbed wire, Claymore mines, standard ground-buried mines, flares, fuses, napalm, white phosphorus. Then a pair of helicopters brought in a Signal Corps team of radio experts. Antennae were erected, guyed in place, and radio sets and a diesel generator put in operation.

A very young looking specialist six walked up to the Special Forces officer and saluted.

"Communications are in, sir," he said.

"What happened to the stuff that was here?"

"I guess the guys who were here blew it just before Charlie moved in," the specialist said. "It's all here, anyway. Charlie would have taken it if it was operable."

"Thanks a lot," the Special Forces officer said. "You might as well head home."

"Colonel, one of my boys wants to stay."

"Does he, now?"

That, Bill thought, seemed to be a very good way to volunteer to get killed.

"He busted out of Ranger School, sir, but he's still hot to trot."

"Well, you know the rules as well as I do," the colonel said. "Only Special Forces."

The young specialist said nothing, just shifted his M–16 over his shoulder.

"Well, if you were to suggest to me that you leave a technician to make sure that stuff works," the colonel said. "I would bow to your professional judgment. Then, if you sort of forgot about him for a couple of weeks, I could maybe say he had on-the-job training."

"Thank you, sir," the specialist said. "I'll go get him."

Bill had expected some crew-cut football-player type his own age. The volunteer was a specialist five in his late twenties, a plump, squat man wearing GI glasses.

"Sir," he said very militarily, saluting, "Specialist Kirchman reporting for duty."

"Can you use that thing, Kirchman?" the colonel asked, pointing at the M–16 automatic rifle.

"Expert, sir," Kirchman said.

"You may have to," the colonel said. "Are you married, Kirchman?"

"Yes, sir."

"And you know what you're getting into?"

"Yes, sir, I think so."

"Lieutenant Leavitt's the team chief. He's that tall thin officer down there loading bodies," the colonel said, pointing. "Report to him. Tell him I said I've approved."

"Yes, sir," the specialist said. "Thank you, sir." He saluted, about-faced, and started off at a trot.

"Kirchman," the colonel called, and Kirchman stopped and turned around.

"Yes, sir?"

"Thank you, Kirchman," the colonel said.

The Special Forces colonel waited until the camp was reestablished, and made a tour of its defenses before turning to Major Kramer and saying, "Any time you're ready, Major." For the first time he seemed to notice Bill, or at least the cane. "What happened to you, son?"

"I had a little wreck, sir," Bill said.

"He's the young buck who flew that shot-up Huey to An Khe last night, Colonel," Major Kramer said.

"Oh," the colonel said. "You're Byrnes. I should have guessed. Well, thanks for the effort, son. We appreciate it." He didn't wait for an answer. He climbed quickly into the rear of Kramer's Huey and matter-of-factly took the crew chief's crash helmet (with its radio communications) away from him. In two minutes, they were in the air, making a low-level pass over the hilltop to give the colonel a last look at the reestablished outpost. And then they quickly gained altitude and flew away.

When they landed, Bill went to the orderly room and collected the proper forms and the official box for Lieutenant Halverson's personal belongings. It took him more than two hours to pack Halverson's things, and to list them on the form: "1 Lighter, cigarette, Zippo," and "6 pair, trousers, uniform, khaki," and "1 ea. Holy Bible" and "1 ea. Kit, toilet, with razor, blades, etc."

It filled, in triplicate, four pages of the prescribed form. He had begun to write the draft of the letter of sympathy for Major Kramer's signature, and had five times gotten as far as "Dear Mrs. Halverson" and quitting, when Captain Hawker walked into the tent.

"How's it going, Gimpy?" Hawker asked.

"I've got his stuff packed," Bill said. "This letter is something else."

"The Old Man had some spare time," Captain Hawker said. "He wants you to see how this sounds." He handed Bill several sheets of paper. "Let me have the summary court forms, and I'll check them while you read that," he said.

Bill unfolded the paper and began to read.

Dear Mrs. Halverson:
By now you have been officially informed of the death of your husband. This letter is both to extend to you the heartfelt sympathy of the officers and men of the 170th Aviation Company in your bereavement, and to provide you with some of the details of the action in which Lieutenant Halverson met his death.

This organization was requested to provide aircraft and aircrews to make an emergency evacuation of a position occupied by Special Forces troops which was in immediate danger of being overrun by vastly superior enemy forces. Because of the hazardous nature of the mission, volunteers were requested.

Lieutenant Halverson was the first officer to volunteer. I consider it a measure of the respect and esteem held for Lieutenant Halverson by his subordinates

that the second officer to volunteer was
Warrant Officer Junior Grade Wilson
Campbell Byrnes III, your husband's co-pilot
and friend.

En route to the area of action, it was
learned that ten members of the beleaguered
garrison had been seriously wounded and
required immediate medical evacuation.  In
the opinion of the officer commanding the
operation, Lieutenant Halverson was the best
qualified officer and pilot to undertake
this most hazardous mission.

In the face of intense enemy automatic
weapons fire, and with total disregard for
his own personal safety, Lieutenant Halverson landed his aircraft so that the
wounded could be loaded aboard.  His courage and professional skill were an inspira-
tion to all who witnessed the action.

While the helicopter was being loaded
on the ground, the enemy brought the landing zone under heavy mortar and machine gun
fire.  An officer with less dedication to
duty would have been wholly justified in
leaving the area.  Your husband chose to
remain, even after the helicopter immediately ahead of him on the landing zone was
destroyed by enemy fire.

Just as the last of the wounded were
placed aboard Lieutenant Halverson's helicopter, a mortar round struck virtually
beside the ship.  Two of the wounded men
in the helicopter and your husband were
instantly killed.

I know that Lieutenant Halverson would
be pleased to know that Mr. Byrnes, although wounded himself, and although the
helicopter had suffered the loss of all its
communications and navigation equipment, was
able to accomplish the mission begun by
your husband.  He successfully flew the
damaged aircraft to a hospital.

Your husband's actions, not only in his
last mission but during all of his assign-

ment to this command, were in the highest
traditions of the military service, and of
the Long Grey Line. He constantly displayed
a wholly commendable devotion to duty, and
enjoyed the respect and affection of his
comrades-in-arms. I am pleased to inform
you that I have just been notified by Headquarters, Military Assistance Command,
Vietnam, of the posthumous award of the
Silver Star Medal to Lieutenant Halverson
for his valor above and beyond the call of
duty in the action which cost his life.

He had previously been recommended for
the Distinguished Flying Cross, and this,
too, will be awarded posthumously.

It seems pertinent, too, to tell you
that all of us were aware of the pride
Lieutenant Halverson took in his family, and
how much of a source of strength you were to
him.

Again, permit me to extend the heartfelt
sympathy of the officers and men of the
170th Aviation Company on the untimely death
of your husband and our friend and com-
rade-in-arms.

Sincerely,

Harrison Kramer
Major, Armor,
Commanding.

Bill didn't read the letter straight through. He was about
halfway through when his eyes watered, and his throat
tightened, and he got up and walked to the door of the tent
so Captain Hawker wouldn't see him. He squeezed his eyes
shut and held his hand tightly over them until he could get
control of himself.

Then he finished the letter. Then he didn't care. He
leaned on the door of the tent and put his hands over his
eyes and wept.

Hawker didn't say anything until Bill had stopped. Then he said, "Good job on the Baron's personal effects, Bill. What do you think of the letter?"

"Not much," Bill said, the words coming out angrily.

"You'd better explain that," Hawker said sharply.

"That's not hard," Bill said. "I have the somewhat unpatriotic idea that Halverson's wife would rather have a flesh and blood father for that new baby than the memory of a dead hero . . . with or without the hearts and flowers and the posthumous pieces of tin."

"He was a soldier. He got paid for driving helicopters. He knew what the score was, just like you and me. Soldiers get killed. That's the name of the game."

"That makes it right?"

"I didn't say that," Hawker said. "I didn't . . ."

"For that lousy little hilltop? Who wants it?"

"What is your solution for the problem of communist expansion, Mr. Byrnes?" Hawker asked. "To give in to fatherly Uncle Ho?"

Bill didn't answer.

"Sometimes, Mr. Byrnes, it is necessary to stand up and get counted. Either as an individual or a country. When a country stands up, it needs soldiers. The Baron was a good soldier. He was trained as a soldier, he fought as a professional, and he died like one. I can think of lots worse ways to buy the farm."

"Such as?" Bill countered, aware and not caring that he was pretty close to insubordination, if indeed he hadn't already crossed that line.

"Such as dying of starvation, or wounds, or being driven out of your mind by fatherly Uncle Ho. You've seen the pictures of those Air Force prisoners, Mr. Byrnes. And you saw, today, what Charlie had done to those bodies."

Bill didn't answer again for a long time, because he was afraid he would say something that Hawker couldn't possibly overlook. Hawker was a pro, like his father. They just didn't understand. Finally, he gained control of himself.

"I'm sorry, sir," he said.

"Forget it," Hawker said, after a moment. "I liked the Baron too." Then he paused, and smiled, obviously on a new subject: "Let's go up to the club. I'll buy you a steak and a drink to celebrate."

The words came out without thought, bitter and angry:

"Just what the hell have you got to celebrate?"

Hawker's face turned stern, and his eyes flashed. Then he gained control of himself.

"Why, since you ask, Gimpy," he said, "and since you apparently haven't noticed my new collar doo-dad, the fact is that I am celebrating the elevation of Mrs. Hawker's husband to a majority."

Bill looked at him. Hawker was wearing the gold leaves of a major.

"I'm sorry," Bill said. "Congratulations."

"Duly accepted," Hawker said. "And a word to the wise, Gimpy. Never pick a fight with a guy who three weeks from now will be your company commander."

"Is the Old Man going home?" Bill asked.

"Uh-huh. And I'll get the company. Sufficient reason to celebrate?"

"Yes, sir," Bill said.

"Let's go, Gimpy," Hawker said. "It's been a long, long day."

## ❀ 8 ❀

THE NAME Gimpy stuck, even after Bill gave up the cane. He spent the next two weeks grounded, running errands for the company. This was somewhat more complicated than the words suggest. One of the errands he ran, for example, was the exchange of three crates full of nonfunctioning aircraft instruments for new or rebuilt instruments. The Army had taken over a World War II pocket aircraft carrier and converted it to a floating helicopter repair base. Bill, riding as a passenger in one Huey, and with a gunship as an escort, spent two days flying to and from the ship, anchored in Cam Ranh Bay, and making the exchange. He also made other trips up and down South Vietnam, ranging from a hurry-up trip to a quartermaster depot to replace a burned-out refrigerator cooling unit for the company mess hall to even less military-sounding — but essential — errands, such as taking his turn as battalion officer-who-goes-for-the-new-movies.

He wasn't anxious to go back into combat, but he did feel a little relieved when the battalion surgeon told him he was certifying him as fit for flight duty, even though he still had a slight limp.

When he left the surgeon's office, Bill went directly to the orderly room. The door to Major Kramer's office was open, and even before he had a chance to speak to the first sergeant on duty, Kramer called out:

"Hail and farewell, Gimpy, come on in."

Bill walked in and saluted. Kramer and Hawker and several of the veteran pilots, commissioned and warrant, were in the room. There was a bottle of bourbon on Kramer's desk, and glasses. Kramer pushed the bottle and a glass toward Bill.

"Just got the orders, Gimpy," Kramer said. "Next week this time, you and Major Hawker will be sort of old-timers. At your age, that's something of an accomplishment."

Bill didn't want the drink, but there didn't seem to be a tactful way to refuse.

"We were just talking about you," Kramer said.

"What did the doc say?" Hawker asked.

"I'm for duty, sir," Bill said.

"In the morning, report to Mr. Gabriel," Hawker said, at the same time pointing with his glass at the warrant officer pilot. "We want to see if you can shoot. Have you any objections to going into the gunships?"

"No, sir," Bill said. "None at all."

"Then make the old school try tomorrow," Hawker said.

"How is the leg, Gimpy?" Gabriel asked. He was an old-timer, but he wasn't much over twenty-one himself.

"I'll limp a while, I guess," Bill said. "But it's all right."

"Up to a parade?" Hawker asked.

"Thank you just the same, sir, but no thank you."

"Sorry about that," Kramer said. "But we are going to have a parade come Thursday, and you, Gimpy, will be there standing tall and straight."

"I know," Bill said, deciding he'd figured it out. "Mac

Vee said there will be a parade, and you've just decided who is outranked by everybody else. Right? And I'm elected?"

"Not at all," Kramer said. "Parades are necessary for good order and discipline and morale and such. Or so I heard. Anyway, we'll all be there. We are going to impress our new draft of junior birdmen with the fact that this is a GI outfit."

Bill didn't know what to think, so he said nothing.

"Old military game of feast and famine," Hawker explained. "After being short of pilots for months and months, we're getting twenty-three — count them, twenty-three — fresh from good old Fort Rucker."

"Which means that all the deserving, like us," Gabriel said, "can go home."

Bill now said what he was thinking. "If we're going to lose that many old pilots, that's going to hurt."

"Sorry about that," Gabriel said.

"Keep a stiff upper lip, old boy," another of the old warrants said, mocking a British accent, "and you'll muddle on through somehow, don't you know?"

There was laughter, but there was truth in what Bill had said, and Hawker answered him.

"We're going to have to do some shifting of pilots, Byrnes, you're right."

And that, Bill thought, is why I'm being given a chance to go into the guns. It was a little premature. He didn't have that much experience. Well, better riding with the guns than having to sit down again in the left seat of a slick. He wasn't sure that he'd have the courage to do that, after the way Halverson had bought the farm. At least in the guns you kept moving. That was easier than sitting helpless on the ground waiting for Charlie to lob in mortar rounds. The guys who got hit in the gunships didn't know about it until the helicopter started coming apart.

He was surprised the next morning when he walked into the briefing room to find out that his post-grounding check ride, his gun-instruction ride, and his gunship check ride were not only to be rolled all into one, on the same day, but that, euphemistically, he was to be given "on-the-job-training."

"Sixteenth Infantry's going to run a truck convoy up Route Fourteen from Kontum to Dak To," Mr. Gabriel said, handing him their flight plan. "We're riding shotgun. We're Number One in a flight of four."

"You're section leader?" Bill asked. That was normally a commissioned officer's job.

"Nobody here but us warrants," Gabriel explained.

"Oh," Bill said.

He was further surprised to see that his name, not Gabriel's, was on the flight plan as pilot. He decided that it was simply because he was taking a check ride. Gabriel could fly it as well from the left seat as from the pilot's, when the time came.

At first, when they cranked the Huey, Bill's leg hurt, but surprisingly, it either stopped hurting or he stopped thinking about it as they went into the air. They flew the few miles from Pleiku to Kontum and landed to confer with the officer in charge of the infantry truck convoy.

With him was a major from First Division Headquarters, who laid a map out on the floor of the chopper and pointed out where his intelligence information indicated the most likely spots for ambush would be. He told them that for three miles on both sides of the highway it was a cleared area. All the civilians had been moved out. Anything they saw moving would be the enemy.

Gabriel said nothing that would indicate that Bill was on a training mission. He said simply that he was the senior warrant officer present, and therefore in command.

"If it's all right with you," Gabriel said, "we'll make a run up there on the deck, a reconnaissance by fire, to see what we can scare up. Then we'll send one ship a half mile ahead of the convoy, and the other three will ride with you."

"You're the experts," the major said. "Do it your way."

"Let's go, then," Gabriel said. "I'm a short-timer. These things make me nervous."

"When do you go home?" the major asked.

"Friday morning," Gabriel said.

"I'll see you on the plane," the major said. They laughed and shook hands.

In the Huey, as they cranked it up, Gabriel said. "You fly. Make irregular S's over the road, maybe a thousand yards on each side."

"Check," Bill said.

Bill saw nothing. But ten miles up the road, Gabriel did.

"There they are," he said. "See 'em?"

"No," Bill admitted.

"Make a three-sixty," Gabriel ordered. "I'll show you."

"I see 'em," the gunner called. "About at the bridge."

Bill made the turn and found the bridge, but saw nothing.

And then he did.

"I've got them in sight," he said. "The fallen trees?"

"Right," Gabriel said, and then pushed the radio transmit switch.

"Three, come in on our tail with rockets, will you? You might as well expend everything. You'll have time to re-arm before bringing the trucks in. But hold off until we see what kind of a shot Gimpy is."

"Roger, Gabe," the radio replied.

"One making pass," Gabriel's voice said. Bill understood this was all the instruction he was going to get. He dropped the nose of the Huey and lined himself up on the freshly fallen trees overlooking the road and the bridge. He touched the machine-gun trigger. From either side of him four machine guns barked. Every fifth round was a tracer. Bill saw where they were striking the ground and adjusted the attitude of the Huey accordingly.

"You're close enough," Gabriel said, matter-of-factly, "Charlie's been known to shoot back, you know."

Bill pulled on the trigger. As he did, he saw the winking of a machine gun, and then another, and then two more. He watched as his tracers moved up to the line of fallen trees. He held the impact point by changing the attitude of the chopper as he neared the target.

"Break to the right," Gabriel ordered.

As soon as the words were out of his mouth, Bill saw the orange flash of the rockets from the helicopter behind them, coming in on their tail. They streaked under him and exploded against the target. It was quickly obscured in smoke.

"That looked pretty good to me, Gabe," the voice came over the radio.

"That got him a gen-u-ine pottery doll. If he does it again, he'll get a simulated straw hat with a band saying 'Souvenir of Palisades Park,' " Gabriel said.

"Another pass?" Bill asked.

"No, the rockets got what was there. Anyway, the tanks'll give it a hosing when they come through," Gabriel reported. "Three, break loose and rearm. Wait for us back there."

"Three breaking," the radio replied, and out of the corner of his eye Bill saw the Huey turn and head back down the highway to Kontum.

They didn't see any other activity the rest of the way to Dak To, nor on the way back. On the return trip, Bill could see where they had machine-gunned and rocketed the ambush site. The vegetation had been leveled, and the rockets had started fires which still smoldered. He thought that he could make out bodies lying crumpled up on the ground.

When they landed, he helped the gunner and crew chief to empty the container which held the fired shell cases, and to replace the ammunition he'd fired.

Number Three helicopter again took off first, and began to describe slow circles as the convoy itself began to move down the road. Two medium tanks and three armored personnel carriers led the column, followed by trucks and every so often another tank, or a pair of personnel carriers. More tanks and personnel carriers brought up the rear. The column extended more than a mile on the narrow road.

It was a tempting target for the Viet Cong.

Before they reached the bridge where they had attacked the Viet Cong on their first pass, the Viet Cong struck again from a place where they had seen no indication of activity before.

It was like watching a set of toy trains and then wondering why one car in the middle of the train had suddenly gone off the track. For that's what happened. All of a sudden, one of the trucks near the head of the convoy simply turned halfway off the road and ran into a tree. The convoy in front of it kept moving, but the rear half was blocked.

"Four, ride over us and spot. We'll take the left, Number Two take the right," Gabriel said, and then, somewhat impatiently, to Bill: "OK, Gimpy, now!"

Bill had no idea what he was shooting at, but picked an imaginary line fifty feet off the road and stitched it with the fire of the eight machine guns. He heard a clicking noise in his ears, and realized that Gabriel was tuning their FM radio to the frequency used by the tanks and armored personnel carriers.

"Twenty yards to the left," a voice said. "Let 'em have the fire."

From the muzzle of one of the tanks in the convoy, flame belched forth, an angry orange line. Immediately, black smoke poured up, as the flaming fuel reached its target. Bill dipped the nose of the helicopter behind a small hill, made a very sharp, steep turn, and then swooped in across the road, firing where the flamethrower had struck.

It was over in less than a minute.

"Hold off in the choppers, we're going to have a look-see," a calm voice ordered from the ground, and as he spoke, Bill saw the infantrymen pour from the back of the armored personnel carriers and disappear in the vegetation toward the burned area.

In a minute or two, there was a report.

"Half a dozen of them here," a voice said. "May be more but they've bugged out."

"Anybody get it?" Gabriel asked.

"The driver of the truck took a slug in the arm," a voice said.

"There's a place up by that bridge where we can get a

Dustoff in," Gabriel said. "You want to send your tanks ahead to clear it?"

"Will do, will you call for Dustoff?"

"Affirmative," Gabriel said. "Be here in four, five minutes." He switched frequency again, and then called: "Dustoff Control, this is Shotgun Zebra."

"Go ahead, Shotgun Zebra."

"We have a slightly wounded at Coordinates George George Oboe Jig George Jig Oboe Oboe. Not serious, but he's got a long ride otherwise. Can you handle?"

"Stand by one, Shotgun Zebra," the radio said. There was a pause. "Shotgun Zebra, Dustoff on the way. Estimate four minutes."

"Roger, Dustoff. Have him contact me on arrival. And thanks muchly."

"Zebra," another voice said, almost immediately. "This is your Dustoff. Where do I go?"

"Dustoff, hold on me. We have to clear the area. Stand by one."

"Dustoff standing by."

"Let's go see what the tanks are doing," Gabriel ordered Bill. The Medical Evacuation Huey — the Dustoff — was approaching from their rear. Bill moved up the convoy, fifty feet off the ground. He came up behind the tanks and saw that they were lacing the previously strafed ambush site with machine guns and cannon.

"You can send the Dustoff," a voice said.

"On the way," the Dustoff pilot answered. "I'll put down on the near side of the bridge."

He fluttered in almost immediately. Bill saw a small knot of men, apparently the wounded man assisted by his buddies, make their way along the edge of the road. And then they had the wounded man in the helicopter and it rose abruptly into the air.

"Thank you, Dustoff," Gabriel's voice said.

"Any time," the voice replied. "But just for your information, we took three hits."

"Roger, Dustoff, thank you for the information," Gabriel said. "Two, clear that area out. Expend everything."

"On the way!" The Number Two ship, like Number Four, was armed with rockets, and swooped in where they had strafed and machine-gunned before.

"Charlie's a great guy," Gabriel said bitterly over the intercom. "He knew that was a Dustoff. He knew that if one of his own wounded was down there, we'd have picked him up. Sometimes," Gabriel said, "Charlie annoys me just a little."

Bill could never remember having heard such bitterness before.

He expected more action, but after the second rocket strafing of the ambush point, the Viet Cong never appeared again. The convoy rolled into Dak To completely intact.

When they got back to the base, and Bill had filled out the flight plan and given it to Mr. Gabriel, he asked him how he'd done.

"Well, for a boy with few brains and an almost total lack of muscular coordination, Gimpy, I'd say you did rather well. One of these days, after you're old enough, they may even give you a license to drive one of these."

He'd passed. He was pleased. He realized now that he wanted very much to be the co-pilot of a gunship.

Major Kramer was as good as his word. There was a parade on Thursday. A Chinook appeared, bringing a band.

A small band, to be sure, but it had a bass drum, two tubas, drums, and enough trumpets to earn the title.

The company was lined up, the new pilots and the new enlisted men looking rather crisp, the old-timers not quite seedy, but definitely like old-timers. A twin-engined Beech-craft showed up from Saigon, and three senior officers got out and were met by Major Kramer.

At that point, the seventeen persons to be decorated found out for the first time that they were persons to be decorated. They were summoned to the orderly room and told where they would stand, now that the secret was out.

"And for those of you who are wondering 'why did Major Kramer wait until now to tell me?' the answer is that Major Kramer is a wise old man, and otherwise you guys would have done Charlie credit, ducking into the jungle. Major Hawker will personally stay with you until you have finished being decorated."

The brigadier general, at that point, had his own little surprise.

"Major Kramer, you will join these gentlemen," he said. "You are to be decorated yourself."

Thirty minutes later, standing in a sweat-soaked, mussed khaki uniform, a little dizzy in the 115 degree heat and 90% humidity, Warrant Officer Junior Grade Wilson Campbell Byrnes III, the sixth officer in the line to be decorated, was invested with the Bronze Star Medal for Valor, the Distinguished Flying Cross, the Purple Heart, and the Air Medal with three clusters.

Major Kramer and two of the enlisted men being decorated fainted from the heat and had to be carried off the pierced-steel planking which served as the parade ground.

The band was out of tune, when it could be heard over the roar of the Air Force jets using the runway. The brigadier general who pinned on the medals stabbed Bill painfully in the breast with the pin of the Air Medal. When, involuntarily, Bill looked down at his chest, he smelled himself. He stank. The four medals, instead of being arrayed in a neat, proud row, hung together, making a tinkling noise. When the men marched off, somewhat out of step, the Purple Heart ripped through the mildew-weakened cloth of Bill's shirt and fell off.

And before the troops were dismissed, an Air Force Caribou came in for a landing. Its left main landing gear collapsed, and the plane skidded noisily down the runway before coming to a rest against a sandbagged revetment and exploding.

One of the warrants in the ranks of those decorated expressed Bill's feelings rather aptly.

"Glory, glory, hall-eee-lou-yah," he said, his voice thick with disgust.

The first thing Bill did when he got back to his tent and stripped off his clothes was to mark off on his calendar the days he had remaining in Vietnam. He didn't feel like a hero. He was tired and dirty and his leg hurt. All he wanted to do in the world was get out of the Army.

In the morning, because he respected Major Kramer, he went down and said good-bye to him as the major got onto the plane that would carry him to Saigon. He said good-bye to some of the others, and was sorry that Gabriel had apparently caught another plane so that he didn't have the chance to say "so long" to him.

As soon as the plane started its engines, Bill started to walk back across the field to the 170th's area. He was intercepted by Specialist Cohen, who had been Major Kramer's gunner.

"How goes it, Cohen?" he said, returning the New Yorker's salute.

"I'm looking for a job," Cohen said.

"What happened to the last one?"

"The major went home."

"I'm sure you'll get another good pilot," Bill said.

"I volunteer. OK?"

"OK, what?"

"Can I be your gunner?"

"You got the wrong guy, Cohen. All I do is go along for the ride."

"You putting me on, Mr. Byrnes?"

"What's this all about?"

"If you don't want me, say so, but level with me, huh?"

"I don't honestly know what you're talking about," Bill said.

"The bulletin board says you're a gunship aircraft commander. And an instruction pilot."

"Now you're putting me on," Bill said.

"So, I'll show you." Cohen led him to the bulletin board in front of the orderly room. It was as Cohen had said. Over Major Hawker's signature was a listing of aircraft commanders, arranged alphabetically. Bill's name headed the list. But it was obviously an error.

"I apologize," Bill said. "But somebody made a mistake. That's wrong. I appreciate your offer, Cohen, and if I ever get a ship, I'd love to have you. But that's wrong."

Cohen looked at him suspiciously, saluted, and said, very formally, "Well, thank you very much anyway, sir."

Bill went into the orderly room.

"Is Major Hawker busy, Sergeant?" he asked the first sergeant.

"I'll see, sir," the first sergeant said, and stuck his head into Hawker's office. "Mr. Byrnes to see you, if you're free, sir."

"I was about to send for him. Send him in, Sergeant, please."

Bill went to the door, knocked, was told to come in, entered, and saluted. A lieutenant was there, one of the new pilots, wearing both aviator's wings and the blue and silver insignia of the Expert Combat Infantryman.

"Bill, this is Lieutenant Rodgers," Major Hawker said. "This is Mr. Byrnes, Lieutenant, the officer I've been talking about."

"How do you do, sir?" Bill said, politely, and then, "I didn't know you were busy, Major. I'd like a minute with you, when you can spare the time."

"I'm free now," Hawker said.

"Somebody goofed," Bill said. "They've got me listed as an aircraft commander and IP."

"No goof," Hawker said. "And your first job is to get Lieutenant Rodgers to the point where he can assume command of the gunship platoon."

"Major, I don't . . ."

"Mr. Gabriel said you were the best qualified of all the people he rode with," Hawker said.

"Sir, you must have misunderstood Mr. Gabriel," Bill said.

"I don't think so," Hawker said.

"Sir, may I request that you check with Mr. Gabriel?"

"That's not possible, I'm afraid," Hawker said.

"Sir, he can't be out of the country yet. We can get him on the telephone . . ."

"No, we can't, Bill," Hawker said, gently. "Gabe was so anxious to get out of here that he caught a ride with an AO–1 that stopped in here last night. They flew into a hill."

Bill just looked at him.

"I guess something was wrong with the altimeter. Or it's proof that you shouldn't fly instruments in an AO–1, or something," Hawker said.

"Or that you can only push your luck so far," Bill said. He felt sick to his stomach. "But that's still got nothing to do with me."

"I'll entertain suggestions," Hawker said.

Bill said nothing. He went over in his mind the names of the pilots with more experience than he had, ones he felt had better qualifications. They had either just gone home, or had other duties. Four had been transferred to the 193rd Aviation Company, which was apparently in worse shape for experienced pilots than the 170th.

"You're it, Bill," Hawker said, finally.

"Lieutenant," Bill said to Rodgers, "I just hope you know what a hell of a lousy spot you're in."

"If things are that bad, Mr. Byrnes," Lieutenant Rodgers said, "the only way they can get is better. Right?"

Bill didn't answer. His answer would have been insubordinate.

"May I go, sir?"

"Sure," Hawker said. "Take Lieutenant Rodgers on a tour of the place."

# ❀ 9 ❀

LIEUTENANT RODGERS did not prove himself to be an apt pilot, or for that matter, an apt student. Even Cohen, who had become their gunner, was aware of this. He never said anything, of course, because that would have been out of place. But he was unable to keep from raising his very expressive eyebrows at what he considered to be Rodgers's more glaring inadequacies.

It was three weeks before Bill turned Rodgers over to Hawker for a check ride. He did it then with mixed emotions. Since there was no qualified officer to command the gunship platoon, Hawker was doing that himself, in addition to his basic duty of commanding the company. Instead of flying alone in the command ship, Hawker commanded the company from the platoon commander's gunship. Sending Rodgers up for his check ride seemed to be the lesser of two evils. Hawker couldn't keep doing both jobs.

Although Bill had gone out of his way to make his relationship with Hawker more formal than ever, now that Hawker was commanding officer, Hawker seemed to be doing the opposite. He came into Bill's tent carrying two cans of beer.

"Let's go where nobody can hear us and philosophize, Gimpy," he said.

When they were at the place where Bill had fired the .45 to satisfy Major Kramer when he'd first arrived, Hawker said:

"Remember the shooting exhibition?"

"Yes, sir," Bill said. "I haven't fired it since."

Hawker abruptly got to the point: "What's wrong with Rodgers?"

"Some guys can fly, some guys can't. He can't. But I think he's a good officer," Bill said.

"Should I give him the platoon?"

"You can't command it forever," Bill said. "And the company at the same time."

"That's right," Hawker said. "I can't. You do the best you can with what you've got. And he's what I've got. I wish you had a commission."

"What for?"

"For the obvious reason."

"Not me, Major. I've got seven months and some days, and then you can have the Republic of Vietnam, the Bell HU–1D helicopter, Tiger-Lily Control, and the entire United States Army as a gift. Wrapped in a bow."

"I think you mean that."

"I have never meant anything more in my life," Bill said.

"The Army's been good to you," Hawker said.

"How the hell do you figure that? The only thing I've learned is that I've got sort of a reverse Midas touch. Everybody I like gets killed."

"That leaves me out of the friendship, apparently," Hawker said.

"You didn't get on the plane to go home yet," Bill said. "If I were you, I'd take out a lot of life insurance. If Halverson's Silver Star was really silver, maybe his wife could get enough out of selling it to buy his baby a pacifier. Now that's an appropriate word: 'pacifier,' to make peaceful."

"How many hours have you flown this month?" Hawker asked.

"I don't know," Bill said.

"Yes, you do."

"Hundred and ninety some," Bill said.

"That's about fifty too many," Hawker said.

"Let's say that I'm building up time to further my military career," Bill said, sarcastically.

"How much of it was IP time for Rodgers?"

Bill didn't answer.

"I asked you a question, Gimpy," Hawker said.

"Forty, maybe. Forty-five."

"OK, it's official. Rodgers is now checked out and in command. You have no further obligation to him in an instructional sense. Understood?"

"Yes, sir."

"Come on, Gimpy," Hawker said. "Let's go get us a drink."

"That's against regulations, sir," Bill said. "I'm not twenty-one. I can't be trusted with booze."

"Consider me your guardian," Hawker said.

"I wouldn't have your job for all the money in the world," Bill said.

"I didn't ask for it," Hawker said. "They gave it to me." He looked at the beer can in his hand. "Dutch used to say that shooting beer cans helped him get rid of his frustrations."

They set the can up on the barbed-wire support pole as they had that first time. It took Bill six shots to hit it, and when he unloaded the remaining round from the chamber, his hands were shaking.

"You get out of practice," he said.

"Yeah, you do," Hawker said. "Let's get that drink."

There was an assault the next morning. A young — in the sense that he was a newcomer — warrant officer pilot reported to Bill to serve as co-pilot. As they were readying the ship for flight, Lieutenant Rodgers came up, self-conscious in his new role as platoon commander. He made a show of inspecting the four machine guns on each side of the gunship.

"Everything all right, here, teacher?" he asked.

"Ready to go, sir," Bill said.

"There's one thing you should know about Mr. Byrnes," Rodgers said to the young warrant. "His bite is worse than his bark."

There was a little awkward laughter at this, then Rodgers spotted Cohen.

"I sort of thought you'd ride with me, Cohen," he said, trying to make a joke of it. "I thought the commanding officer always got you."

Cohen looked at Bill and there was fear in his eyes. It was obvious that he didn't want to ride with Rodgers.

"Lieutenant," Bill said, "Cohen and I have been together a long . . ."

"I wasn't sure you wanted me, Lieutenant," Cohen said. "I'd like to ride with you."

"You don't mind, Mr. Byrnes?"

I mind like hell, Bill thought. And Cohen's scared to death. But we can't say it.

"If you're willing to take the worst gunner in the outfit, Lieutenant, you're welcome to him."

Cohen had a minute alone with Bill before he trotted over to Lieutenant Rodgers's Huey. He said, "Do me a favor, will you? Talk him out of me. But gently."

"I'll fix it, Cohen," Bill said, with a confidence he didn't feel.

An hour later, Lieutenant Rodgers and Specialist Cohen were dead. Charlie had a .50 caliber air-cooled machine gun well hidden and well placed. Rodgers was in Number One position on his first pass. In Number Three position, Bill saw the muzzle flash, and then watched the heavy tracers as the gunner corrected his aim and sent the orange blurs into Rodgers's engine. At the worst possible time, when he was making a steep bank and breaking to the right, Rodgers's engine quit. He tried to make an autorotation and failed. The helicopter hit on its nose, turned over and rolled, and then burst into flame.

"I'll take that gun," Bill said to the others in the flight. He made a sharp, dangerously sharp, bank to the left, and then, a hundred yards from the enemy gun, opened up with all eight machine guns, jockeying the helicopter so he'd have more time on target and at the same time making a better target of himself. The stream of bullets tore up the area. There was no return fire. Even so, he kept firing until there was simply no more ammunition.

Only then did he become aware of Hawker's voice on the radio.

"This is Tiger-Lily One. Flaming-Lily Three, have you expended ordnance?"

"Affirmative," Bill said.

"Flaming-Lily Three, break off and return to base to rearm. There is a mission for you."

"Roger," Bill said. "Flaming-Lily Three, breaking off."

As Hawker's voice ordered the rest of the flight to form on him, Bill wondered what else Hawker had for him to do.

He quickly rearmed and waited for further orders, forcing himself not to think either of the crashed Huey or of Cohen's frightened face when last he saw it. But no further orders came, and he couldn't raise Hawker on the radio when he called.

He had just about decided that the day would be capped by Hawker buying the farm when he saw Hawker's Huey come fluttering in alone, to hover and land beside him.

He got out, and walked to Bill's window.

"Have your crew chief shut it down and fuel it up," he said. "Meet me in my office in five minutes."

"Yes, sir," Bill said. "What's up?"

"I'll tell you when you get there, Mr. Byrnes," Hawker said, and walked quickly away.

Major Hawker wasn't at the orderly room when Bill got there, but the first sergeant told him to go in and wait, that he would be along shortly. As Bill went into the inner office, Master Sergeant Gowald came bouncing into the orderly room.

"How goes it, Mr. Byrnes?" he asked, jovially.

"Ginger-peachy," Bill said. "Just ginger-peachy."

Gowald didn't reply.

Bill settled himself on the homemade couch and waited for Hawker, standing up when Hawker finally came in.

"Oh, sit down," Hawker said, somewhat disgustedly. Then he sat down behind his desk.

"What do we do now?" Bill asked. "We just killed Rodgers, you know that? And I personally killed Cohen."

"How do you figure that?"

"Cohen didn't want to ride with Rodgers at all. I let him."

"Did you order him to ride with Rodgers?"

"No," Bill said, and then he started to cry, and didn't care. "He was my friend, Cohen. All I had to do was tell Rodgers that Cohen rode with me, and he wouldn't have gone with him."

"I'll tell you what you did do," Hawker said. "You almost killed your co-pilot, and your gunner, by that childish display of angry and insane flying to knock out that machine gun."

"I don't think I like that," Bill said.

"Sorry about that," Hawker said. "But it's the truth."

"So what are you going to do with me? Send me to Vietnam and make a chopper pilot out of me?"

"Shut up," Hawker said. "Just shut up." He waited until Bill said, "Yes, sir," before going on:

"I just checked some records around here, Gimpy," Hawker said. "You have flown not about one hundred and ninety hours so far this month, but, to be precise, two hundred fifteen and one half. Plus what you flew today."

Bill shrugged.

"I have just talked to Battalion, and you're on your merry way to Hawaii on Rest and Recuperation leave. That'll look better on your records than combat fatigue."

"Quite aside from the fact that I don't want an R and R," Bill said, "and wouldn't go to Hawaii if I did, I don't really much care what you put on my records. Just between us, Major."

"And when you come back from R and R, bright and bushy-tailed, you will assume command of the gun platoon."

"Not me. I'm a warrant type officer. No command responsibility."

"Your application for a direct commission will be approved."

"I didn't apply for a commission," Bill said. "And I've got no intention of applying for one."

"What I'll do, after you're gone, is to call up the CO and say that you forgot to sign it before you left, and would it be all right if I signed it for you," Hawker said.

"I won't take it, Major, I mean that."

"I hadn't realized how far over the edge you'd slipped, Gimpy, or maybe I didn't want to," Hawker said. "But I'll spell it out for you. I failed in my responsibility when I let Rodgers fly as aircraft commander, much less command that platoon. *I* got him killed, and *I* got Cohen and the others killed. And you failed in your responsibility by standing idly by."

"My responsibility to whom?"

"To yourself," Hawker said. And then he raised his voice. "Sergeant Gowald!"

Gowald came through the door without knocking.

"Sergeant, I wonder if you would be good enough to see that Mr. Byrnes gets packed for R and R and gets over to Base Ops as soon as possible? They're holding a Saigon plane for him."

"Be glad to, sir," Gowald said. "Come on, Mr. Byrnes."

"I don't want to go on R and R," Bill said.

"Come on, Mr. Byrnes," Gowald repeated, and he put his hands on Bill's arms. Bill's first thought was that Gowald was entirely capable of carrying him right out of the office. Then he thought that maybe he was losing his mind. Only a nut would refuse an R and R.

"I can make it by myself, Sergeant," he said. "Thank you."

"I'll just go along and see what I can do to help," Gowald said gently. He didn't take his ham of a hand off Bill's arm.

The Saigon-Honolulu flight was known as the Commuter's Express, because the great majority of its passengers were married men, going to Hawaii to meet their wives, who joined them there from the States. The bachelors usually headed for Tokyo or Hong Kong or Bangkok when their turn for a leave came up.

Bill slept most of the way to Honolulu, more tired than he realized. He felt rather foolish when the plane landed and he seemed to be the only man aboard without a wife to greet him emotionally. As he walked through the airport, he saw half a dozen West Point cadets in uniform come through and head for the taxi stand.

It took him a full minute to adjust to this, before he remembered that it was leave time at the Academy and these were cadets coming home. It was absolutely incredible to realize that if things had followed his father's plan he would have been among them.

He got in a cab and went out to his mother's apartment. She threw her arms around him and wept a little and said he had lost weight, and then she asked:

"Is your father with you?"

"No," he said. "Why?"

"Well, maybe I shouldn't say . . . I suppose I shouldn't."

"Shouldn't what?"

"I sort of asked your father if he couldn't arrange for you

to have your R and R's together. You didn't know about it? Would it hurt your feelings?"

"Mother, it would," Bill said. "But believe me, he didn't have a thing to do with me coming on R and R just now."

"I'm sure he didn't, dear," his mother said, and he thought: she's putting me on.

"Mom," he said. "It's been a long flight. Would you mind if I went to bed?"

"I should have thought of that," she said. "I'm sorry."

He wasn't sleepy. He just didn't want to talk to her, and that was the only way he could think of getting out of it without hurting her feelings. He lay down, sure that he wouldn't get a minute's sleep, and almost instantly fell asleep and slept through until ten the next morning. When he got up, he put on slacks and a loud Hawaiian shirt.

His mother was obviously as happy as she had been in some time, and certainly much happier than she had been when he had passed through on the way to Vietnam. Part of it, of course, was that he was home. Another part of it was the telegram on his breakfast plate:

MRS. W.C. BYRNES JR
1507 THE ILIKANAI
HONOLULU HAWAII

ARRIVING ALONE PAN AM FLIGHT 330 1630
HONOLULU TIME.  LOVE CAMPBELL.

He thought his mother had a great talent for self-deception. The "alone" business was meant to tell her that he wasn't coming with Little Billy in tow. His mother interpreted it to mean that General Byrnes knew Bill was already in Honolulu.

"Well, how would you like to spend the day until Dad gets here?" she asked, with great enthusiasm. She thought everything was going to be fine and pleasant again. That the family was together and bygones would be bygones.

"Mother, why don't I just go lie on the beach or something, and take it easy and let you arrange things for Dad?"

"You've forgotten," she said. "We always have dinner out when Dad comes home."

"I'd forgotten," he said.

"But you go to the beach, dear, that's a good idea. Or why don't you take the car and go for a drive?"

"Thank you," he said.

He walked a while on the beach. Then, nervous and hungry for something to do, he went to the garage and took the car and started driving. He thought about Cohen and Halverson and Rodgers, and about Hawker and his stupid idea of giving him a commission.

He didn't realize where he was heading until the MP at the gate of Schofield Barracks waved the car through and saluted. He returned the salute automatically.

What I want now is a beer, he decided. He drove to the Officer's Open Mess and very deliberately parked in the general public parking area, rather than in the space marked RESERVED FOR GENERAL OFFICERS.

He went first to the swimming pool. His hunger for a beer had shifted to a hunger born of memories of the girls at the club pool in their bathing suits. He would do both. He would get a beer and watch the girls. And think.

He saw a prime example of the latter ordering a Coke and a hot dog from the poolside stand. Blonde and well tanned. Very nice, he decided. She caught him looking at her and eyed him with what could have been either interest or distaste. In some embarrassment, he said to the attendant:

"Let me have a can of beer, please."

"Uh . . ." the attendant said, and Bill looked at him. "Excuse me," the attendant said, "but aren't you General Byrnes's son?"

It was the bartender who knew his mother.

"Yes, I am," Bill said.

"Gee, I'm sorry," the attendant said. "But the club officer himself said that no cadet's supposed to get anything at all with alcohol in it."

Bill felt an unreasoning anger.

"Well," he said, "by all means, let's keep the club officer happy and the Corps of Cadets sober."

He felt his hands shake and recognized that as a sign of tension. Then he heard someone snicker. That was too much. He walked away without saying anything else, and, almost blindly, walked to the far side of the pool and sat down on the edge of a wooden and canvas sun chair.

The wave of anger frightened him. It reminded him of that stupid exhibition he'd put on knocking out the gun that had gotten Rodgers. Hawker was right. That was stupidly angry. And he had been stupidly angry here, too. He had no reason to jump on the attendant.

Hawker had used the phrase "combat fatigue" and Hawker had said Bill had "slipped over the edge."

Had he?

Hawker didn't bandy words like that around loosely. Hawker chose his words as Bill's father chose his. Hawker meant what he said.

A can of beer held in a tanned female hand appeared at the edge of the pool, and then a female head in a bathing cap.

"Gimpy?" the face asked.

I *am* losing my mind, Bill thought. I never saw this woman before in my life and she's calling me a name that only a few people know.

"Yes?" he said.

"That fat and lazy old man over there," the woman said, "thought you might need this, and sent me over with it."

Bill looked across the pool. Captain Chedister, the battalion adjutant, obviously himself on R and R, smiled and waved a lazy hand.

Bill waved back.

"He heard what the bartender said about people under twenty-one," the woman said. "I'm Mary Chedister." She shook his hand when he took the beer. "Come on over after a while if you want another one."

"Tell him 'thanks,'" Bill said. "And Gimpy thanks you, too."

"Gimpy's welcome," the woman said, and let herself fall backward with a splash into the pool.

He was halfway through the beer when the blonde in the tan and the bikini came over, and sat down beside him.

"I suppose you think you're smart, Billy," she said.

"Who are you?"

"Jeanne Hawthorne," she said. "We were in Berlin together."

"What are you doing here?"

"My father runs the place," she said. "And your father's in Vietnam but due in here."

"Good," Bill said. He now remembered her father. He had apparently made general.

"Unless you ruin everything by being a smart aleck about the beer."

"All I'm doing is quenching my thirst," he said. "You know, the first law of survival."

"Don't be so smart," she said. "What if your tactical officer saw you?"

His "tac officer"? That was cadet lingo. Then all of a sudden he understood. She hadn't heard about his leaving West Point. Well, professionals didn't talk about things like that in polite company or before young girls. He drained the beer can and tossed it into a waste can, where it made a large racket. Jeanne frowned.

"What are *you* doing here in sunny Hawaii?" he asked. "Besides getting that attractive tan?"

"Well, I'm going to the University," she said, "and tonight I'm going to the Cadet Hop. Are you?"

"I hadn't thought about it," he said. "But I don't think so."

"Your folks and mine were supposed to have dinner tonight," she said, "but I guess it got put off because you came in."

"Because I came in?"

"With the cadets," she said. "You're an Army brat. The cadet dance is where the parents auction off the family females."

"I'd forgotten," he said.

"What did they do to you at West Point?" she said. "Brainwash you?"

"They tried," he said, "but I have managed to remain unwashed."

"Well, at least you've changed from when I last knew you," she said. "You were stuffy and proper then."

"You like the change?" he said.

"Come to the dance tonight and find out," she said. "It's nice to see you again, Billy." She walked away. He liked the view. He watched until it was apparent that she was leaving the club as well as the pool and then walked over to where Captain Chedister sat sprawled.

"Hello, Gimpy, you juvenile delinquent, you," he said. "You want another beer?"

"I'd love another beer," Bill said.

"Go get him a beer, dear," he said to his wife, "and send him down the primrose path."

She smiled and got up and got the beer, and when she came back, she said, "The bartender said something before about General Byrnes — or am I prying?"

"He's my father."

"I didn't know that, Gimpy," Chedister said.

"Kramer knew. He didn't say anything."

"I'm the original clam," Chedister said. "But before I clam up, give your dad my congratulations. I never had a chance to congratulate a general before, even secondhand."

"What for?"

"He just got his third star. Didn't you know?"

"No. I just got in."

"Yeah, come to think of it, you're not due for R and R until next month sometime."

"Major Hawker said I was flipping," Bill said. "He said it would look better if I took an R and R instead of getting combat fatigue."

"A couple of days in the sun with a blonde, and you'll be good as new," Chedister said. "Ask me."

Bill laughed, and then he saw the forced smile on Mary Chedister's face and decided that he had no right to intrude on Chedister's R and R. He finished his beer, refused a third, and left. He drove around the island killing time until he was sure that his mother would have left to meet his father at the airport, and then he went home.

# ❀ 10 ❀

HE GOT a key for the apartment from the desk, and opened the door himself. Halfway down the corridor, he found himself face to face with his father. They both stopped, and looked at each other.

"Hello, Billy," his father said. "How are you?"

"How are you, sir?"

"I got in a couple of hours early," his father said. "Since you had the car, it was necessary for me to ride in a cab."

Bill didn't reply.

"I'm sorry, I didn't mean that," his father said.

"Forget it."

"I'm fixing myself a drink. Do you want one?"

"Please."

His father turned and Bill followed him silently out onto the balcony. His father poured liquor into two glasses.

"I don't know how you take yours," he said. "I'm not used to your being an officer."

"With water, please," Bill said. He didn't want the drink, but he understood that it was as close to a gesture of conciliation as his father was likely to come.

"Thank you," he said, when his father handed him the drink.

"To being home," his father said, raising the glass in a toast.

"To being home," Bill said.

"How's your war, Billy?" his father asked.

"Lousy, how's yours?"

"I'm out of it. I'm going to STRIKE Command in Florida as Chief of Staff."

"I heard about the promotion. Congratulations. And congratulations from Captain Chedister, too."

"Who's he?"

"He's our adjutant. He just got me a beer out at Schofield when the bartender decided I was still a member of the Corps of Cadets."

"Any regrets about that? About the Point?"

"Only that it made you mad," Bill said.

"I'm over that," his father said. "You're not in trouble are you, son? Is that what you meant about a lousy war?"

"No, I'm not in trouble. Except that they put me on R and R rather than write me up for combat fatigue."

"Bad up there?"

"I lost a friend of mine day before yesterday. A specialist from the Bronx named Cohen. Good kid. And I lost my temper."

"How did he get it?"

"I guess you could say nobly. He went as gunner for an officer we both knew was incompetent, and he was."

"That's a strong accusation," his father said. "Incompetency."

"That's the way it goes," Bill said, meeting his father's eyes. His father looked very much like Hawker, come to think of it. A little less hair. Bigger bags under the eyes.

"Why are you looking at me that way?"

"You look like a friend of mine . . . Like my commanding officer."

"I was looking at you, too," his father said. "You've changed."

"I'm almost certifiable as a battlefield nut," Bill said. "Is that what you meant?"

"You still have a big mouth, but no, that's not what I meant. I meant you have matured."

"Let's say I've had a couple of good, screaming scares."

"That does it sometimes," his father said. "That, and the assumption of responsibility for other men's lives."

Bill just looked at him.

"Shall we call a truce while we're here?" his father asked. "I'd like to negotiate a permanent peace, but I'll settle for a truce."

"Agreed," Bill said, and put out his hand. His father shook it.

"Thank you," his father said, "and I would now like to ask a favor of you."

"What?"

"We're going to dinner tonight at Schofield. I know your mother would like you to wear your uniform. I suspect that she's wholly aware of the reasons advanced by gossiping women for your leaving . . . school. And I think it would be nice if you wore your uniform. And your decorations."

"Yes, sir, I'll wear it."

"Thank you," his father said.

His mother appeared then with a tray of cheese and crackers.

"I thought you might be hungry," she said, "and . . ." she looked between them.

"I've missed these," his father said. "Your mother has a knack for spreading cheese on crackers. When it comes to something complicated however, like frying an egg . . ."

The three of them laughed together. Her relief was almost visible.

After a while, she sent General Byrnes in to get dressed, saying he'd have to pin his own decorations on. It was patently obvious to both of them that she wanted to be alone with Bill, but the general went willingly.

"I know how you feel about the Army, son," she said, "but I want to ask you to do me a favor."

"What's that? You sound like a recruiting officer."

"Men sometimes gossip as much as women, Billy, and I'm sure your father has heard all sorts of reasons advanced . . . everything but the real one . . . why you left West Point. I'm sure it would please him very much if you would wear your uniform tonight. Out at Schofield, especially. Have you got any ribbons?"

"I'll go in full uniform, Mother," Bill said.

"I'm so glad you're not at each other's throats again."

The only reason Warrant Officer Junior Grade Byrnes had a dress white uniform at all was because he had been given the option of buying either summer or winter dress uniform at Fort Rucker. The white summer uniform had been much cheaper than the winter, and he wasn't planning on being around the Army long enough to wear dress blues.

Now it came in just right.

Mrs. Byrnes had neglected to call the Officers' Open Mess for reservations for three, but in the case of a newly promoted lieutenant general fresh from Vietnam, arrangements are easily and smoothly made in any officers' club. A brigadier general (the junior one) was discreetly moved to a table reserved for a colonel, who in turn moved to a table just vacated by a lieutenant colonel and so on down the line until one more table was moved into the anterooms reserved for lieutenants and warrant officers, who didn't notice the difference, and Lieutenant General W.C. Byrnes and party were shown to a table on the dance floor.

"Two sour mash bourbon and water, and a Manhattan for Mrs. Byrnes," the general ordered. It was the same bartender, but this time he didn't question the age of the general's son.

Major General Hawthorne, the commanding general, was the first to come by the table to offer General Byrnes congratulations on his promotion.

"You remember Bill, of course, General?" Bill's father said.

"Why, yes, of course," General Hawthorne said. "Nice to see you again, Bill. I thought you were at the Point."

"He's been in Vietnam flying gunships," General Byrnes said, with a quiet pride. "And rather well, to judge by that fruit salad."

"Do you plan to go back to the Point?" Hawthorne asked. It was a natural question, but, to judge by the look on General Byrnes's face, it was the worst possible question he could have asked. Bill saw his father stiffen, and then with an effort relax.

"I'm being commissioned," Bill said. "As soon as I get back to Vietnam. I don't think I'll go back to the Point, sir."

"Of course not," his father said, rising to the occasion. "The important thing is the command of troops. We can teach Bill to read and write later on."

"I know some officers who've done remarkably well

without being able to do either," General Hawthorne said, laughing. "Jeanne's here tonight, Bill. Why don't you go over to the table and say hello?"

"Thank you, sir, I will," Bill said. He got up and excused himself and walked over to the other table. Her tan against the white dress looked even better than it had against the bathing suit.

There were, as the unofficial custom dictated, a half dozen cadets paying court to the general's daughter. Bill tapped the nearest on the shoulder.

"Excuse me, mister," he said, in his best West Point diction. "This is my dance with the lady."

"Certainly, sir," the cadet said, and came to a brace.

The general's daughter broke tradition. Instead of a demure and ladylike "I'd love to dance," she looked at him and said, "Billy, I ought to push you in the pool." But she got up, and they danced.